ZHUGE LIANG LEGEND
AND RESCLUSIVE RESEARCH

WHITEWATER WU

About the Author:

Whitewater Wu is a distinguished author and former editor-in-chief of a prominent newspaper. A literary figure with deep expertise in both poetry and fiction, Whitewater Wu is also the Chief Editor of the Modern Chinese Great Dictionary. His contributions to the literary world span multiple genres and languages, establishing him as a notable voice in international literature.

Among Whitewater Wu's accolades is the first prize for his novel Anecdote Editing, awarded by the "Weekend" competition. His novel The Critic was selected as a textbook in the Chinese-English Translation Tutorial published by Tsinghua University Press, solidifying his role as an educator and cultural bridge.

Whitewater Wu's extensive literary career reflects a commitment to both his native Chinese heritage and a global literary audience.

• Table of Contents •

Brief Introduction

-- Decision-making in the Tent, Winning from Thousands of Miles Away

Zhuge Liang was the incarnation of wisdom known to every Chinese people. " Decision-making in the Tent, Winning from Thousands of Miles Away." Burn Bowang Hillside with fire; arguing heatedly with scholars; using the straw boat to get the arrow; borrowing east wind; thrice defeated Zhou Yu; arranged stone fortress cleverly; Seized Meng Huo seven times; the empty city stratagem... Left behind the wonderful stories one after another.

At the end of the Eastern Han Dynasty, there were frequent wars. Zhuge Liang and his brothers took refuge in Jingzhou (Xiangyang) with his uncle Xuan and cultivated in the wild.

Whether Zhuge Liang's seclusion and cultivated land were in Longzhong of Hubei province, China, or Wolong Hillock of Henan Province, there's been a lot of controversy in modern times. The author of this book has revealed the latest secrets and put forward detailed and convincing solid evidence.

Chapter 1 - Famous Figure Zhuge Liang

Zhuge Liang (181-234 AD), style name Kongming, alias Wolong (means "lying dragon"), was born in Yangdu County, Langya Shire, Xuzhou (now Zhuge village, Zhuanbu Town, Yinan County, Linyi City, Shandong Province) at the end of the Eastern Han Dynasty. He was the Prime Minister of the Shu Han Dynasty during the Three Kingdoms period, an outstanding politician, strategist and inventor.

The Zhuge family belonged to the first class with good reputation. Zhuge Feng, his ancestor, was once a division captain at the Yuan Emperor of the Han Dynasty. His father Zhuge Gui was the county magistrate of Taishan in the late Han Dynasty, and his mother's surname was Zhang. The couple gave birth to three sons and two daughters: Zhuge Jin, the first son; Zhuge Liang, the second son; Zhuge Jun, the youngest. Zhuge Liang also had two elder sisters. Zhuge Liang's father died when he was eight. Zhuge Jin, Zhuge Liang's eldest brother, studied the Ru theory when he was young so as to be renown for his filial and piety. Later, to evade chaos he went down to Jiangdong (the east of Yangzi River) and was reused by Sun Quan (Dongwu Emperor). He

was gradually promoted to the highest military general in the Dongwu Dynasty. Zhuge Jun, Zhuge Liang's younger brother, was rarely recorded in the history books. It was said that he followed Zhuge Liang all the time, and later he became a military officer in Shu Kingdom. in the Shu regime (Shu, one of the Three Kingdoms). Zhuge Liang had a cousin, Zhuge Dan, who served as an important military and political position in the Wei regime (Wei, one of the Three Kingdoms). In this period, not only did the Zhuge family came forth outstanding in large numbers, but also they were all in power in three hostile regimes, which was extremely rare in Chinese history. Undoubtedly, the most dazzling star among them was Zhuge Liang.

Zhuge Liang's childhood was extremely rough, and his parents died in succession when he was very young. Later, all the brothers and sisters were raised by their uncle Zhuge Xuan. Zhuge Liang's childhood was the time when the Eastern Han Dynasty was extremely corrupt and people were in a state of poverty, and natural disasters continued to occur, and many people suffer hunger and cold, cornered, finally in 184 A.D. the outbreak of the Yellow Turban peasant uprising. When Zhuge Liang was 9 years old, Dong Zhuo, a powerful man in Xiliang, led his troops to the capital to abolish the little emperor and set up another emperor to control the Eastern Han regime. Other ambitious powerful bandits started to fight one after another under the pretext of attacking Dong Zhuo. Since then, it began the chaotic period of mighty division and warlord battle. When Zhuge Liang was 13 years old, Cao Cao attacked Tao Qian, who occupied Xuzhou at that time, making Zhuge Liang's hometown face the disaster of destruction. In order to avoid the war, Zhuge Xuan led Zhuge Liang, Zhuge Jun and Zhuge Liang's two elder sisters to trek half of China, to take refuge Liu Biao in Jingzhou governor in Xiangyang. The teenager Zhuge Liang left his hometown, not only witnessed, but also experienced the disaster of the chaotic era. He was eager for stability and unity. He was determined to fight to eliminate the tyrants and to reconstruct the unified country.

At that time, Xiangyang was the capital of Jingzhou. Jingzhou governed Nanyang, Southern Shire, Jiangxia and the other seven shires, which were equivalent to the current Hubei Province, Hunan Province, the south of Henan Province, and part of Guangdong Province and Guangxi Province. Therefore, Xiangyang almost became the political, economic and cultural center of the southern half of China at that time, people were in a rich life with well-developed culture and education. At the same time, Xiangyang was also an important post road connecting the north and the south. Han River connecting the East and the West also gathered and crossed here. Xiangyang had become an important water and land transportation hub, thus becoming the information center where it's easy to get to know the world's major events quickly.

Zhuge Xuan, Zhuge Liang's uncle, and Liu Biao, the governor of Jingzhou, were close friends. When their family came to Xiangyang, they were taken special care of by Liu Biao and soon established a close relationship with local famous families. Zhuge Liang got to know Pang Degong, Huang Chengyan, a famous scholar in Xiangyang, Sima Hui, Kuai Liang, Kuai Yue, etc. so in this way it broadened his vision, increased his knowledge and layed a foundation for his future career. Zhuge Liang lived inside the city after his arrival in Xiangyang and studied in the school in the south of the city. Zhuge Liang's elder sister married Pang Shanmin, the son of Pang

Degang, a respected man of high reputation in Xiangyang; Pang Tong, who was known as Fengchu, was Pang Degang's nephew; Zhuge Liang's other elder sister married Kuai Qi, a member of the big Kuai family in Xiangyang; Zhuge Liang's wife was the daughter of Huang Chengyan, a famous man of Xiangyang; his mother-in-law and Liu Biao's wife were cousins; Cai Mao was Zhuge Liang wife's uncle, who was in charge of Jingzhou army logistics. at that time. Undoubtedly, all these social relations had played an important role for Zhuge Liang in his acquisition of various kinds of knowledge.

When Zhuge Liang was living and cultivating in Longzhong, he had four very close friends: Xu Shu, Shi Tao, Meng Jian, Cui Jun, who were collectively called "four friends of Longzhong". Xu Shu, a renowned figure in the history of the Three Kingdoms, in the beginning, he assisted Liu Bei. Later, because his mother was tricked in house arrest by Cao Cao, he had to turn to Cao Cao. Such as "His body is in Cao Camp, but his heart is in Han Camp", "Xu Shu entered the Cao Camp- - Without a word" and other popular sayings showed his state of mind to Liu Bei and Han Dynasty. His loyalty and filial piety became a model for later generations. Shi Tao, Jingzhou famous person, after Liu Cong was surrendered, he was recruited by Cao Cao to be an official of Wei, and finally became a prefecture governor and a military officer. Meng Jian, a famous man in Jingzhou, was also recruited by Cao Cao to be an official in Wei after Liu Cong surrendered to Cao Cao. Finally, he was sent to the governor of Liangzhou and also to be a general in the East. Cui Jun, a famous man in Jingzhou, after Liu Cong surrendered to Cao Cao, disappeared mysteriously, no more information was recorded in history. Maybe he didn't want to work for Cao Cao and went to the mountains to cultivate his mind. According to the records of Wei Strategy, when Zhuge Liang and Shi Tao, Xu Shu and Meng Jian who traveled to Jingzhou to study, Zhuge Liang once said to the three："You three can be governors." He meant to tell them that they could get the rank of governors in the future. When they asked Zhuge Liang how big an official he could be, Zhuge Liang laughed but didn't say a word. With the world in his heart, he naturally had a broader field of view.

At the age of 17, his uncle Zhugexuan died. He moved out of Xiangyang City and settled down in Longzhong mountain in the west, read a lot, made friends with scholars, and paid close attention to the situation of the country. He once compared himself with Guan Zhong and Yue Yi, he determined to devote himself to the reconstruction of a strong country. Zhuge Liang studied hard and paid attention to the world. He had read many books, such as the Confucian works "Poem", "Book", " Book of Rites", "Spring and Autumn", etc. He had also read the books of strategists, such as "Zuozhuan", "Warring States Strategies", "Sunzi's Art of War", etc. In particular, Zhuge Liang's famous Eight-array map (the Eightfold Maze) evolved from his study of previous military works. Zhuge Liang absorbed the nutrition of these theories, but he did not blindly believe in them. He once remarked about the philosophers: " Laozi was good at nourishing personality, but couldn't face danger; Shangyang was good at policy, but couldn't be enlightenment; Su and Zhang were good at poetry, but couldn't make an alliance." He met with Xu Shu, Shi Tao, Meng Jian and others in the school, who were "closest friends", they were often discussing world affairs together, and they determined to reform politics.

The unique objective environment nurtured Zhuge Liang, who had the spirit of the elite. After his own diligent study, Zhuge Liang soon had the talent to be great leaders and he was known as "Lying Dragon". In 207 AD, Liu Bei, in a desperate state but with anbitious mind, came to Longzhong thrice to visit Zhuge Liang. Liu Bei asked Zhuge Liang for advice on how to unify the country and invited Zhuge Liang to come out of the mountain to help him complete the great cause of the reunification. Zhuge Liang analyzed the situation of the country incisively from the

Zhuge Liang tomb at the foot of Dingjun mountain, Mianxian County, Hanzhong City

aspects of politics, military affairs, geography and personnel. He suggested that Liu Bei would occupy Jingzhou and Yizhou as the base areas; would establish good relations with the ethnic minorities in the southwest; and would form an alliance with Sun Quan, who occupied the lower reaches of the Yangtze River, to fight against Cao Cao who had unified the north with a strong force. He would build up his own political theory, accumulate his strength and wait for the right time; when the time came, Liu Bei's army can attacking the Central Plains from both sides of Jingzhou and Hanzhong, in order to achieve the goal of unifying the country and revitalizing the Han Dynasty. This was the famous Longzhong Strategies. Since then, history had proved that this was a correct strategy with farsightedness.

After Zhuge Liang was invited by Liu Bei to leave Longzhong, he assisted Liu Bei to establish Shu Han regime. After the establishment of the Shu Han Dynasty, Zhuge

Liang was appointed the prime minister and Wuxiang Marquis. Zhuge Liang started to manage the government affairs, at the beginning he assisted Liu Bei and later Liu Chan, he actually became the real leader in politics and military affairs of the Shu Han Dynasty. His strategies were in two aspects. Inside of the regime: To care for the people in the country, to observe etqiuette, to restrain officials, to use power with caution, to be sincere, to be fair. Outside of the regime: to connect with Wu (one of the Three Kingdoms) and together to oppose Wei. In the 12th year of Jianxing in Shu Han Dynasty (234 AD.), he died in Wuzhangyuan (now in Qi Mountain, Baoji City, Shaanxi) during the fifth Northern Expedition, and was buried in Dingjun Mountain (now Southeast of Mianxian County, Shaanxi Province), at the age of 54. Liu Chan conferred Zhuge Liang as Zhongwu Marquis. Zhuge Liang's ability and character were highly respected in later generations, so later generations often called Zhuge Wu Marquis and Zhuge Marquis. He and Liu Bei, Emperor of Han Dynasty, promoted famous generals and capable ministers and laid a foundation for the reign of Shu Han. Because of his military ability, the Eastern Jin regime especially bestowed on him as Wuxing King. Zhuge Liang's representative works of prose included: the Strategy Guide, the book of admonition and so on. He invented the wooden cow and stray horse, Zhuge Liang lantern, etc., and transformed the crossbow, which was called Zhuge crossbow. One crossbow could produce ten arrows at a time. Because Zhuge Liang had outstanding talent and noble character at the same time, the later generations had a high evaluation of Zhuge Liang, who was the symbol of loyal officials and wise people in traditional Chinese culture.

Zhuge Liang had never returned to Longzhong's former residence since he accepted Liu Bei's invitation in 207 AD. In 208 AD, Cao Cao led his troops to attack Jingzhou, and Liu Bei was defeated in Xiakou (now Hankou). At the time of being defeated and in danger, Zhuge Liang set out to the Easten Wu and formed a Sun-Liu Alliance, which won the battle of Chibi and made Liu Bei occupy the four shires of Jingzhou. In 221 A.D., the Shu empire was founded, and Zhuge Liang was Prime Minister. After Liu Bei's death, Zhuge Liang enforced the rule of law, made friends with Sun Quan and fought in the South and the North until he died in the front line of the northern expedition.

Although Zhuge Liang didn't realize the long-cherished wish of unifying the country, he made contributions to the development of Southwest China and the reunification of the country through unremitting efforts. His intelligence, dedication, and spirit for doing his best till his own heart ceased to beat had always been respected and praised highly by people, leaving a profound impact on later generations.

The common people in the Shu Han area had a deep memory for Zhuge Liang. The records of the Three Kingdoms were written: "Up to now, people in Liang and Yi regions still missed Zhuge Liang." After Zhuge Liang's death, "The people of Shu state thought of Zhuge Liang and admired his intelligence. As long as the Shu government did good things for the people, although it was not advocated by his son, Zhuge Zhan, the people all publicized that it was advocated by Zhuge Liang's son." It could be seen that Zhuge Liang was very loved by the people because of his outstanding governance ability and noble moral character. People in Shu always had the habit of mourning Zhuge Liang spontaneously.

People at that time, including the enemy state of Cao Wei, praised highly of Zhuge Liang. Zhuge Liang was widely respected and loved by officials and ordinaary people in the Shu Han Dynasties. Qiao Zhou did not agree with the northern expedition, but after Zhuge Liang's death, he first went to mourn to express his condolences. Assistant Minister Ji Han praised him for "loyal and wise, dedicated and strategic, liason of Wu and Shu, I'm sorry that he didn't realize his lofty ideals and high aspirations." After Zhuge Liang 's death, the imperial court did not set up a temple, but the people would worship Zhuge Liang spontaneously every year. In terms of the enemy state: Jia Xu evaluated Zhuge Liang as a good statesman; Fu Gan as " Zhuge Liang knows how to govern and

deal with the changes, he is upright and strategic"; and Sima Yi as "a genius in the world". In the war of Wei had defeated Shu, when Zhong Hui entered the middle of the Shu Han Dynasty, he ordered the soldiers were forbidden to cut wood beside Zhuge Liang's tomb and he also paid worship to him in person. People in the Eastern Wu also highly valued Zhuge Liang. Zhang Yan made a detailed comparison between Zhuge Liang and Sima Yi, the two great heroes of the time, praised Zhuge Liang was a great man.

Most of the rulers, ministers and generals of later generations had highly valued Zhuge Liang, especially for his outstanding political and military talents and noble character. There were a lot of poems praising Zhuge Liang in Tang and Song poems. Du Fu's poems "He died before accomplishing his ambition, how can heroes not wet their sleeves with tears"; "Three kindoms praised his honor, welknown for his Eight-array map"; Li Shangyin's poem "Apes and birds are still hesitant to dare to approach, and they still seem to be afraid of Zhuge Liang's strict military orders; the winds rise and the clods flow, gathering and changing, as if for a long time to protect the barracks barriers.of the ancient time"; Lu You's poem "Report Before Departure was well-known. Who can be as devoted as Zhuge Liang to lead the national army to the north of the Han Dynasty and to the Central Plains" and so on were all famous saying. Zhuge Liang was popular at all levels of the society.

Zhuge Liang had two 27-year phases in his life. The first 27-year before 207 AD was the preparation stage for his self-cultivation and determination to contribute to the world. He did not go to Cao Cao in the north or return to Sun Quan in the south, but he assisted Liu Bei, who was "not famous, and with less followers". This was not by accident. He was an orthodox thinker who upheld feudal principles and upheld Confucian loyalty and morality, so he chose to help revive the Han Dynasty. The second 27-year was from 207 to 234 AD, which was the period of Zhuge Liang's loyalty to Shu Han. He was trusted by both the first and the second emperor. He didn't completely abide by the Confucian doctrine. He respected the king but didn't advocate to fight with the Barbarians. He marched into the south and appeased the Barbarians. He carried out the best national policy in the Three Kingdoms. He strictly enforced the law, strictly required justice, formed an alliance with the Dongwu, and strictly governed the army. He fought to the end of his life with the selfless dedication of "Do own best, until the death of life". His spirit of loyalty to the public and the country was deeply loved by Shu people before his death and respected by later generations for a long time. It had become a heritage of traditional Chinese culture.

Chapter 2 - Zhuge Liang Legend

"The Romance of the Three Kingdoms" was adapted from the historical book " Records of the Three Kingdoms", formerly known as "popular romance of the Three Kingdoms."

It was well known that "romance of the Three Kingdoms" had a great influence on Chinese society. Unique popularity brings unique charm, making it one of the most influential works in Chinese classical literature. A large number of plots in The Romance of the three kingdoms were well-known and widely used in various aspects. Zhuge Liang had also become the recognized wisdom incarnation of the Chinese nation.

There are many historical novels in China, but they could not compare with the " Romance of the Three Kingdoms." The "Romance of the Three Kingdoms" was loved by the masses and enriches the spiritual life of the Chinese people. There were many fictional elements in the "Romance of the Three Kingdoms." There are fabricate as well as reality. There were fabricated in the real, and there were also real in the fabricate. But the main line of history and the main historical facts were true. Although there were fabricated and exaggerations in the middle, but their boundaries were not destroying the main historical facts.

The novel was particularly brilliant in its war scenes and war strategy. The rich wisdom contained in these war strategies not only truthfully records the wisdom of the Chinese nation, but also develops on the basis of inheriting the wisdom of the nation. In addition, there were also many folk legends about Zhuge Liang among Chinese people.

Here were some legends about Zhuge Liang:

1. Burn Bowang Hillside with Fire

Liu Bei thrice visited his cottage, Zhuge Liang agreed to help Liu Bei. From spring to autumn, Zhuge Liang joined Liu's barracks as a military division for about half a year. During this period, there was no war in Jingzhou, he mainly focused on defense. He gathered and practiced troops and horses, waiting for the right time, he did not show anything extraordinary. Except for Liu Bei and several famous people's unreserved trust and respect for Zhuge Liang, some people had doubts about his distinguished talents, and some of the soldiers in the camp had doubts about Zhuge Liang.

Cao Cao at Guandu and warehouse pavilion victory, and after pacification Hebei, decided to go back to the south to eradicate the threat located behind. Liu Bei was forced to flee to Jingzhou to join Liu Biao after his defeat in the battle of Rang Mountain. Liu Bei, who was appreciated by Liu Biao, was entrusted with the task of guarding the north of Jingzhou and stationed in Xinye, Nanyang.

One day, a mounted scout horseman came to inform that Cao Cao sent Xia Houdun as the main general, Yu Jin, Li Dian as vice-general, and led the 100,000 armies to force Nanyang Xinye. Before the expedition, Xun Yu, Cao Ying's counselor, said: "Liu Bei was a hero, and Zhuge Liang was a military division, so we should not underestimate the enemy." However, XiahouDun boasted: "Liu Bei and Zhuge Liang were incompetent mediocre people. This time I'm going to catch both of them alive."

Every day Guan Yu and Zhang Fei saw Liu Bei gave Zhuge Liang a special treatment as respectful as a teacher, they were dissatisfied. Because of Zhuge Liang's young age, they thought that he was in vain. Although Liu Bei said: "I have Zhuge Liang, just like the fish have water." Guan and Zhang stopped talking because they respected their brother, but they refused to respect the military adviser Zhuge Liang who had just arrived. Guan Yu and Zhang Fei were dissatisfied with Liu Bei's treatment of Zhuge Liang as his teacher 's etiquette. They had a negative attitude in the face of the war. When

Zhang Fei heard that Xiahou Dun led troops to come, he said to Guan Yu, "Cao Army is here, and it's time to send Zhuge Liang to meet the enemy." Liu Bei asked his two younger brothers about their plans to meet the enemy. Zhang Fei said, "Why don't you send Zhuge Liang to fight the enemy?" Liu Bei criticizes Guan Yu and Zhang Fei and said, "Zhuge Liang uses his wisdom. You two showed your bravery. How can you not accept the task at will?"

Liu Bei hurried to please Zhuge Liang came to discuss countermeasures. "The art of war of Sun Zi" said: "The best way to use troops is to conquer the hearts of the enemy, capture the city is an inferior strategy; the best way is to use your heart to win, use your soldiers to win is an inferior strategy." Zhuge Liang said, "I'm afraid Guan and Zhang will not listen to me. If you want me to use the army, please borrow the seal sword. " Liu Bei gave him the sword. Zhuge Liang then called all the soldiers to listen to the order. Zhang Fei said to Guan Yu, "let's see how he arranges."

Zhuge Liang began to gather many generals and March. Zhuge Liang ordered: "there is a mountain on the left side of Bowang, which is called Yu Mountain; there is a forest on the right side, which is called An Forest, our troops can ambush there. Guan Yu led 1,000 soldiers to ambush in Yushan Mountain. When the enemy arrived, let him go instead of fighting. Their army provisions certain be in the back. If you see the fire in Nanshan, you attack and burn their army provisions. Zhang Fei led a 1,000 soldiers to ambush in the valley behind An Forest, As long as you see the fire in the south, you send your troops to set fire to the old grain store of Bowang city. Guan Ping and Liu Feng lead 500 soldiers to prepare things for fire attack. You wait on both sides after Bowang slope. When the enemy soldiers arrive at the beginning of the watch you set fire. " Then he ordered to send someone from Fancheng to call back General Zhao Yun as the front vanguard, to lead the old and the weak, to command him to lose not win, to feign defeat and retreat, to lure Xia Houdun into the narrow road of the mountain forest; and sent Guan Ping, Zhou Cang, Liu Feng and other people to infiltrate into the rear of the Cao army, burning materials, and causing Cao army panic. In the end, Zhuge Liang said to Liu Bei, "You're leading an army as a backup. All departments must follow my plan, and there must be no mistake."

"We all went out to kill the enemy. What do you do?" he asked. "I only sit in the county seat," said Zhuge Liang. Zhang Fei said with a laugh, "we are all going to work hard, but you are sitting at home, sir, how to enjoy you are!" "The sword seal is here, whoever disobeys the order will be beheaded!" said Zhuge Liang

Liu Bei then said to Guan Yu and Zhang Fei at this time, "don't you know that ' decision-making in the tent, win victory outside the thousands of Li? You must not disobey the military order." Zhang Fei went out with a sneer. Guan Yu said to Zhang Fei, "let's see if his plan is right or not. We'll come back and ask him later."

All the generals did not understand Zhuge Liang's strategy. Although they listened to the order today, they were still confused. Zhuge Liang said to Liu Bei, "You can lead the troops to stay at the foot of Mount Bowang Hillside today. Tomorrow evening the enemy will arrive, and you leave immediately. When you see the fire, turn around and attack them. With MI Zhu and Mi Fang, I led 500 soldiers to guard the county town." He also ordered sun Qian and Jian Yong to prepare for the celebration feast, and arranged for the record of merits to wait for the victory of the army.

Zhuge Liang military deployment completed, not only some officers and men did not know his military strategy, feel suspicious, Even Liu Bei, who worships him all the time, doesn't know the magic of it, he was half believe and half doubt.

This time, Xia Houdun and Yu Jin had arrived at Bowang, their half of the elite soldiers as the forward and the rest doing their best to protect grain wagons. They were on their way, when they suddenly saw the troops rushing over, Zhao Yun was the leader. Xia Houdun ordered Yu Jin and Li Dian to hold back, and laughed: "Xu Shu praised Zhuge Liang as a divine counselor in front of Prime Minister Cao. Now I see his deployment. It's like letting their dogs and sheep with our tigers and leopards fight. I must catch Liu Bei and Zhuge Liang alive." After saying that, let the horse go forward and fighting with Zhao Yun. Less than a few rounds of killing, Zhao Yun pretends to lose and let Xia Houdun catch up with him. Zhao Yun ran away more than ten Li. Suddenly, a gun ring and Liu Bei rush out. Xia Houdun didn't pay attention to these men at all. He said that he would never stop fighting if he didn't straight kill reach to Xinye today, so he urged the army to move forward. Liu Bei and Zhao Yun only retreat.

By this time, it was late, with thick clouds and no moonlight; the night wind was blowing, and it grew stronger and stronger. Xia Houdun only urged the army to move forward. When he arrived at the narrow area of the two mountains, Li Dian and Yu Jin suspected that they would face fire attack and so they ordered the troops to stop-go forward. At this time, they heard the voice of the rear, which shocked the sky. Suddenly, there was a flash of fire and caught up with the strong wind. The fire became more and more prosperous. Soon, the reeds on both sides of the road were also burning. For a moment, all sides were fire. Cao's army was in chaos, trampling on each other and dead countless people. At this time, Zhao Yun leads the troops turns around to pursue and kill, and Xia Houdun suddenly went out at the risk of fireworks. Seeing the bad momentum, Li Dian hurried back to Bowang city and was stopped by an army in the fire. It was general Guan Yu killed it came back. Li Dian ran away in the melee from the path. Xia Houlan and Han Hao came to save army provisions. They met Zhang Fei. Zhang Fei stabs Xia Houlan off his horse and Han Hao escapes. They didn't receive the army until dawn. Cao army was killed and injured countless by the fire, and was attacked by many ambush soldiers.

Everywhere only saw blood and bodies. Xia Houdun gathered up the remnant army and fled back to Xuchang.

Zhuge Liang accepted the troops. Under Zhuge Liang's dispatch, Liu Shire won the battle with a flying flag, and all officers and soldiers appreciated Zhuge Liang's strategy. Guan Yu and Zhang Fei were so impressed that they met each other and sighed, "Zhuge Liang is really a hero! "People saw Mi Zhu and Mi Fang cluster round a small car came here with their troops. There was a person sitting in the car . It was Zhuge Liang with a feather fan and a silk towel. Liu Bei's army returned after a great victory. At this time, Guan Yu and Zhang Fei admired Zhuge Liang's intelligence. Seeing Zhuge Liang, they dismounted and bowed. After a while, all troops came to Xinye. They shared the spoils with the officers and men. When the troops returned to Xinye, Xinye people have been on the road to welcome. Someone said, "it's because Liu Zhijun got the help of the wise people that we all have a safe life! "

Xinye small town resists the 100,000 tiger division, which seems to be an impossible task. However, due to the well used of time and land, it had created another war miracle that uses fewer to defeat the many. Zhuge Liang's chopper small scale, with the help of Bowang Hillside's fire, burned all the doubts of the enemy and even allies about Zhuge Liang's talent, and his reputation of the resourceful since for resourcefulness has since spread far and wide. The reason why he could win was not only that he had no equal in wisdom, but also that he had an accurate grasp of people's hearts. Zhuge Liang expected that his soldiers would not obey the military order, so he invited Liu Bei's sword seal to sit in the town. He anticipated that the general of Cao Wei despised the enemy, carelessness, so he deliberately showed his weakness, lured the enemy into his own hinterland and defeated them at one stroke.

Zhuge Liang used his troops for the first time. He was clever and clever. His crafty plan, won a great victory, a famous battle, Liu Bei and his men greatly admire, layout their own prestige. Guan Yu, Zhang Fei and so on were all in admiration.

After that, Cao Cao shifted his focus to Yuan Tan and Yuan Shang in the north and had no time to take Liu Bei on Jingzhou into account, so that Liu Bei's army could have a chance to recuperate. Liu Biao was unwilling to fight Cao Cao in the north and there was peace in the south of the Central Plains for several years.

2. Arguing Heatedly with Scholars

At the end of the Eastern Han Dynasty, Cao Cao in a way that coerced the emperor to order the princes. Most of the powerful warlords were eliminated by him, only

Liu Bei and Sun Quan still have the possibility of development and expansion. Cao Cao knew that it was difficult to annex these two forces at once. Therefore, Cao Cao sent people to take his letters to the Dongwu and pretends wanted to join forces with Sun Quan to eliminate Liu Bei.

Most of the counselors under Sun Quan advocated to surrender Cao to protect himself, only Lu Su advocated uniting Liu to resist Cao. Zhuge Liang in order for uniting Sun Quan fought against Cao Cao, he took a small boat, A feather fan in hand, a silk kerchief on the head, and alone walked with Lu Su across the river in the bright sunshine to the peach red and willow green land of Dongwu.

At that time, Sun Quan stationed troops in Chaisang Shire, Jiangdong. When he heard that Cao Cao's army had arrived in Xiangyang and wanted to attack Jiangling, he summoned advisers to discuss the strategy of defending the enemy.

In the war of words with Zhuge Liang, there were a group of famous scholars, there were more than 20 people, one of the most famous was Zhang Zhao, all of whom were famous for their resourceful. They wear all the clothes for formal occasions. Zhuge Liang met them one by one and asked their names.

Zhang Zhao and others, seeing Zhuge Liang's spirit floating and distinguished-looking, expected to lobby, so they first asked Zhuge Liang.

Zhang Zhao asked, "I heard that when you lived in seclusion in Longzhong, he compared himself to Guan Zhong and Yue Yi. I don't know if this is true?"

Zhuge Liang replied, "well, it's just a little metaphor of my life."

Zhang Zhao asked, "it's said that Liu Bei thrice visits your cottage, then lucky enough to get your help in. He also said that he felt like a duck to water when he has you. Liu Bei. But now he has even been driven away by Cao Cao from Jingzhou, where he is stationed. What's your plan in the future?"

Zhuge Liang replied: "in my opinion, it's easy to seize the land of Jingzhou, but Liu Bei is the master of benevolence and justice, and he can't bear to seize the territory of Liu Biao. When young Liu Cong, he listened to the sycophant and surrendering to Cao Cao in secret, which make Cao Cao powerful. Not long ago my master Liu Bei garrison Jiangxia, it is because there are bigger plans, not ordinary people can understand."

Zhang Zhao still asked: "in this way, compared with Guan Zhong and Yue Yi, you seems to have different words and deeds. As we all know, Guan Zhong helped Duke Huan of Qi to dominate the princes, and Yue Yi helped the weak state of Yan to capture more than 70 cities of Qi. Both of them have the ability to help the world and manage the country. They will also fight for the common people all over the world and exterminate the unruly scoundrels. But in fact, Liu Bei is able to win some battles and occupy some cities before he got you. Now Liu Bei is defeated by Cao Cao and fled everywhere, leaving Xinye, Fan City, Dangyang and fled to Xiakou. There is no place to live. Why is it that Liu Bei is not as good as before after he got you?? Is Guan Zhong and Yue Yi like this?"

Zhuge Liang smiled dumbly and replied, "my master Liu Bei lost the battle in Runan before, and he temporarily relied on Liu Biao. At that time, his army was less than 1,000, with only Guan Yu, Zhang Fei and Zhao Yun as generals. The Xinye occupied by Liu Bei is only a small county, with fewer people and less food. Liu Bei just lives there temporarily, and will not really dominate with Xinye as a small place. Even so, Xia Houdun and Cao Ren were terrified when we defeated the vanguard forces of millions of Cao's army with the help of poorly equipped and

short of grain. Presumably, Guan Zhong and Yue Yi's use of troops may that's also all it is. And it's common for soldiers to be outnumbered and lose for a while. In the past, Han Gaozu was defeated by Xiang Yu many times and finally defeated Xiang Yu

completely in the next battle, which was the result of assisted by Han Xin who as such true strategic hero. It's not like some boasters sitting at home talking, no one can match them, but they can't think of any way to make a plan on the battlefield. That's what makes people all over the world laugh."

Zhang Zhao was speechless. One by one, the seven counselors who came on the stage later challenged Zhuge Liang, all of them have been retorted by Zhuge Liang to be speechless, with a look of shame on their faces.

At this time, someone in the seat wanted to ask Zhuge Liang a question. Suddenly Huang Gai, the grain inspector, came in from the outside and said in a sharp voice, "Zhuge Liang is a genius in the world. It's not a rite of respect for guests that you can't face each other with your lips. Cao Cao's army has arrived at our border, you do not discuss the strategy to defeat the enemy, just here show off your eloquence!" Huang Gai said to Zhuge Liang, "why don't you tell your good ideas to our master

Sun Quan?"

Zhuge Liang said, "They asked me harsh questions, and I have to answer them."

Zhou Yu also rushed back to Chaisang County to pay a formal visit to Sun Quan. Lu Su had the best friendship with Zhou Yu, so he informed Zhou Yu of all the discussions in these two days. Zhou Yu asked Lu Su to rest assured that he would invite Zhuge Liang to meet him first to discuss the issue.

Zhang Zhao and other dovish who advocate conciliation, Cheng Pu, Huang Gai other hawkish who advocated resistance, they together visit Zhou Yu. Zhou Yu was perfunctory. In the evening, Lu Su and Zhuge Liang to visit Zhou Yu and asked him if he would fight Cao Cao with Liu Bei. Zhou Yu said: "Cao Cao is playing the emperor's signboard. He has great potential. We will lose when we fight. I made up my mind to persuade our lord Sun Quan to surrender." Lu Su immediately argued with Zhou Yu. But Zhuge Liang was secretly sneered at the side.

Zhou Yu asked Zhuge Liang why he laughed. Zhuge Liang said, "I laugh at Lu Su's ignorance of current affairs. I have away, as long as two people, can teach Cao millions of troops to withdraw." He added: "Cao Cao built the bronze sparrow platform. He has long wanted to get two gorgeous beauties, big Qiao and small Qiao. Just send away these two beauties to Cao Cao, and Cao Cao will surely retreat." Zhou Yu was furious and scolded: "Cao Cao, an old thief, he bullied us too much!"

Zhou Yu said, "you don't understand that Daqiao is the wife of general Sun Ce, and Xiaoqiao is my wife." Zhuge Liang pretended to be panic-stricken and said he shouldn't talk nonsense. Zhou Yu was stimulated by Zhuge Liang, and then he said his sincere words: "I am just trying to test. Actually, I wanted to break Cao Cao for a long time, and I also asked you to help me." Zhuge Liang agreed.

The next morning, Sun Quan came to the royal court to discuss the matter. After analyzing the favorable conditions for the war in the Dongwu Dynasty, Zhou Yu said, "I'd like to fight for the general to kill the enemy. I'm afraid that the general won't make up his mind." As soon as Sun Quan heard this, he pulled out his sword and cut off a corner of the table. He said, "Whoever dares to bring up the matter of demoting Cao again will come to an end like this table!"

Sun Quan gave the sword to Zhou Yu. On the spot, he named Zhou Yu as the chief inspector, Cheng Pu as the deputy general, and Lu Su as the commander of the Zan army. He announced to all the officials in the civil and military fields, "Whoever disobeys the order will be killed in accordance with the military law. I've made up my mind. I don't hesitate anymore. We can start the army and destroy Cao Cao at once!" So Sun Quan asked Lu Su to decide to inform the following officials of culture and military affairs, and then arranged Zhuge Liang back to the Posthouse for a rest.

3. Using Straw Boat to Get the Arrow

Cao Cao led the army to try to conquer Dongwu, and Sun Quan and Liu Bei joined forces to fight against Cao. Sun Quan had a general named Zhou Yu, who was both intelligent and brave, but had a narrow mind and was very jealous of Zhuge Liang's ability.

Zhuge Liang was well aware of Zhou Yu's intentions and strategies. Zhou Yu heard that Zhuge Liang already knew that he had taken advantage of Jiang Gan to kill Cai Mao and Zhang Yun. More and more, he felt that he could not let Zhuge Liang alive. Otherwise in the future, it would be great harm to Dongwu. But if he killed Zhuge Liang, he was afraid of being laughed at by Cao Cao, so he tried to find a way to get rid of him.

One day, Zhou Yu gathered together the general to discuss matters under his account and asked Zhuge Liang, "in recent days, we are going to fight against Cao Cao. What weapon will be used first to attack the war when fighting by water?"

Zhuge Liang said, "above the river, bow and arrow will be the first."

Zhou Yu said, "what sir said fits my mind perfectly. But our army is short of arrows. May I ask Monsieur to make 100,000 arrows to kill the enemy? This is an official business, please don't refuse."

Zhuge Liang said, "I don't know when the governor will use these 100,000 arrows?"

Zhou Yu said, "in ten days, can we do it?"

Zhuge Liang said, "Cao Cao will soon attack over, if we wait for ten days, will miss our important chance."

Zhou Yu asked, "Sir, you need a few days to finish?"

Zhuge Liang said, "only three days, I can hand in these 100,000 arrows."

Zhou Yu was surprised and said, "there is no joking in the army."

Zhuge Liang said with a smile, "I want to write a military warrant as a credential. I am willing to be punished if I fail to complete the task within three days. I'll start building arrows tomorrow. On the third day, you can send 500 men to carry the arrows back from the river."

After Zhuge Liang left, Lu Su said to Zhou Yu, "100,000 arrows, how can they make in three days? Is what Zhuge Liang said a lie?"

Zhou Yu shook his head: "he said it himself. I didn't force him. I will give orders to the craftsmen of the army, that they may tarry on purpose, that they may not prepare for him all the materials for making arrows. When it doesn't work out, convict him, and he has nothing to say. You go to investigate and see what he's going to do. Come back and report to me."

Lu Su came to see Zhuge Liang, and Zhuge Liang said, "You need to lend me 20 ships, each of which requires 30 soldiers. The ships are all covered with green cloth, and each ship is bound with more than 1,000 grass targets. I have my own good use. On the third day, there were 100,000 arrows. Just can't let Zhou Yu know, if he knows, my plan will fail."

Lu Su reported to Zhou Yu that he didn't mention borrowing the boat. He only said that Zhuge Liang didn't use arrow bamboo, feather, glue paint and other things. He had his own reason. Zhou Yu was puzzled and said, "I want to know how he explains it for he didn't finish the task in three days!"

Lu Su privately allocated 20 clippers, each of which was equipped with 30 soldiers. According to Zhuge Liang's words, he arranged the green cloth curtains and straw targets, waiting for Zhuge Liang to dispatch. On the first day, there was no movement of Zhuge Liang; on the second day, there was still no movement of Zhuge Liang; until 1 a.m. on the third day, Zhuge Liang secretly invited Lu Su to his boat. Lu Su asked him, "what do you want me to do?" Zhuge Liang said, "please come with me and get the arrows back

together." Lu Su asked, "where can we get it?" Zhuge Liang said, "You don't have to ask. You'll know it when we get there." Zhuge Liang ordered twenty ships to join together with long ropes and head for the north bank.

That night, the fog was all over the sky, and the fog was heavy on the river. People could not see clearly on the opposite side. Zhuge Liang urged the ship to move forward. By 3 a.m., it was close to the water stronghold of Cao Cao. Zhuge Liang ordered the bow of the ship to the west, the stern to be in the East, and the soldiers were hiding in the green cloth curtain. Then he ordered the soldiers on the ship to beat drums and shout loudly. Lu Su was shocked. "What if Cao Cao's soldiers come out?"

Zhuge Liang said with a smile: "the fog locks the river. I don't think they dare to come out. We only drink and have fun here, and go back when the fog is over."

Lu Su dumbfounding, where there is thought to drink, he became restless.

Cao Cao's camp heard drums and shouts, and Yu Jin hurriedly reported to Cao Cao. Hearing drums and shouts, Cao Cao ordered, "there is a lot of fog on the river. The enemy suddenly attacks. We do not see the real situation. Don't go out easily, only let the Bowman shoot at them and keep them away." Then he sent people to another camp to call Zhang Liao and Xu Huang, each with 3000 soldiers with bows and arrows, to rush to the riverside to help the battle.

Soon, more than 10,000 archers put the arrows in the river together, some of which were like rain, some of which fall into the water, some hit the ship's straw targets. The ship was slowly leaning to one side because it got a lot of arrows. Zhuge Liang looked at the wine pouring out of the cup, and command turned the bow. The bow of the boat was facing east and the stern of the boat was facing west. He also ordered his soldiers to beat drums and shouted, and approached the Cao army's water stronghold to receive arrows. It was not until the sun rose and the fog began to disperse that Zhuge Liang ordered the ship to return immediately. By this time, the straw targets on both sides of the twenty boats were covered with arrows. Zhuge Liang ordered all the soldiers on the ship to shout: "thank you for the arrow of Prime Minister Cao!" When a soldier in Cao's army reported this to Cao, Zhuge Liang's ship had returned more than 20 Li, and Cao's army could not catch up with it. Cao Cao regretted it very much.

Zhuge Liang went back to the boat and said to Lu Su, "there are about five or six thousand arrows on each boat. No cost Soochow a little strength, get more than one hundred thousand arrows. Tomorrow can use it to shoot the Cao army, it is not very convenient?"

Lu Su said, "Sir, you are so divine! But how do you know that there is a heavy fog over the river today?"

Zhuge Liang replied: "as a general, if he is not familiar with astronomy and geography, strange gate, yin and Yang, array chart and military potential. That's mediocrity. I speculated three days ago that there is heavy fog today, so the three-day limit is set. Zhou Yu asked me to finish it in ten days. The Craftsman, materials are not ready for me, he is obviously trying to kill me. But my life is given by Heaven, Can Zhou Yu kill me?" Lu Su obeyed.

When the ship arrived at the shore, Zhou Yu had sent five hundred soldiers to wait by the river to carry the arrow.

Zhuge Liang asked the soldiers to pick up more than 100000 arrows from the ship and moved them to the barracks. Lu Su came to see Zhou Yu and narrated Zhuge Liang's use of the straw target on the boat to get the arrow.

Zhou Yu was shocked and sighed: "Zhuge Liang is clever. I'm not as capable as he is!"

4. Borrowing East Wind

On the eve of the battle of Chibi, Zhou Yu was ready to launch a fire attack to burn down Cao's warships and defeat Cao Cao.

Zhou Yu ignored one thing at that time. He didn't expect that the fire attack had a high demand for the wind direction. In the middle reaches of the Yangtze River in the winter, there was more northwest wind than southeast wind. If they want when scraping the northwest wind set fire to Cao's army, Because Cao's army was in the upwind, the northwest wind would not burn Cao's army. Instead, it would burn his own Dongwu army. Zhou Yu couldn't think of a way. He fell ill all of a sudden. Lu Su asked Zhuge Liang to come to the doctor.

Soon, Zhuge Liang came to see Zhou Yu. Zhou Yu said: "My leader Sun Quan sends someone to urge me to March. I observed yesterday that Cao Cao's water stronghold is neat and orderly, and nonidle people can attack it. I thought of a trick. I don't know if I can."

Zhuge Liang said, "don't say it first, but write it in your hands to see if we think the same."

Zhou Yu was very happy. Write, two close looks, Zhou Yu hands was a "fire" word, Zhuge Liang hands was also a "fire" word.

When Zhou Yu saw this, he thought to himself: Zhuge Liang was really a God and a man! But he turned worried into joy and said, "The war is urgent. I hope you can help me."

Zhuge Liang said: "although I am not talented, I once met a man with strange skills. He taught me the heavenly book of the Daoist magic door, which can summon the wind and rain, which means I can do anything I want. If you want to have a southeast wind, you can build a platform on Nanping mountain, called Seven Star altar: nine feet high, three floors, surrounded by 120 people, hand lifting banner streamers. How about I approach things on the stage, borrow three days and three nights of southeast gale to help you use his troops?"

Zhou Yu said: "don't say three days and three nights, as long as there is one night can accomplish our great things. Now the situation is imminent, please do not delay."

Zhuge Liang said, "On the 20th of November I began to call for the wind, until the 22nd to let the wind stop, can you?"

Zhou Yu was very happy. When he got up, he immediately sent 500 strong soldiers to Nanping mountain to build the altar. 120 people were assigned to hold the flag to guard the altar and wait for the order.

Zhuge Liang came to the altar on November 20, bathed and fasted, dressed in Daoyi, barefoot and hair, and ordered the soldiers to guard the altar: "do not leave the place  without permission. Don't talk to each other. Don't make irresponsible re marks casually. Don't make a fuss. Those who disobey the order will be beheaded!" All took orders. Zhuge Liang ascended the altar slowly, see exact direction and location, burned incense in the furnace, poured water in the basin, and looked up to the sky and wished. Zhuge Liang ascends the altar and descends the altar Thrice in one day, but there was no strong wind.

Zhou Yu and others were waiting for the southeast wind in the main military account. Huang Gai and other officials had prepared 20 fireboats. In Cao camp, Zhou Yu's assistant, Gan Ning, and other officials, who were in Cao Army's camp, entangle their water commander to drink in the stronghold every day. They didn't send a person to the shore to patrol. They were surrounded by soldiers and horses of the Dongwu Dynasty. They were all surrounded by people. The soldiers were all rubbing their hands and waiting for the order on the account.

That night, the sky was clear and the wind did not move. Zhou Yu said to Lu Su, " Zhuge Liang's words are absurd. Where is the southeast wind in the winter?"

Lu Su said, "I don't think Zhuge Liang is a fallacy."

Near 11:30 p.m., suddenly listened to the wind, flags fluttering. When Zhou Yu went out to see it, he saw that the flag horn had really drifted to the northwest, and the southeast wind was blowing suddenly. Zhou Yu said in astonishment, "this man has the method of seizing heaven and earth and creating nature, and the skill of ghosts and gods! If we keep him, he will be the bane of Dongwu. Kill him as soon as possible, so as not to worry about the future." Hurriedly called the two generals Ding Feng and Xu Sheng. The secret order said: "take 100 people each. Xu Sheng will go from the river, Ding Feng will go from the dry road to the Seven Star altar on Nanping Mountain. No need to ask more, catch Zhuge Liang and immediately behead him. Bring his head to see me for receiving a reward." Two generals take orders and leave.

Ding Feng's cavalry arrived first. He saw a flag bearer standing in the wind, but not Zhuge Liang. He asked and the flag bearer answered, "Zhuge Liang went down to the altar just now."

At this time, Xu Sheng arrived. The soldier reported, "there is an express ship stopping at the front beach last night. Just now I saw Zhuge Liang get on the boat in his hair, and then the boat went upstream." Ding Feng and Xu Sheng rushed to catch up with each other. Xu Sheng calls to hang up the full sail and caught up with the wind. Finally, he saw that the ship in front of him was not far away. Xu Sheng shouted at the bow, "don't go, military adviser, please!"

Zhuge Liang stood at the stern of the boat and said in a loud voice, "go back and tell your general Zhou Yu. Make good use of this wind to break the Cao's army. I return to Xiakou for a while and meet you again on the other day."

"You stop for a moment, please," said Xu Sheng. "It's important."

Zhuge Liang said: "I already had expected in advance that Zhou Yu can not tolerate me, so I asked Zhao Yun to pick me up in advance. Two generals don't have to chase."

Xu Sheng saw that the boat ahead was not sailing, so he just went ahead. When it was near, Zhao Yun stood on the boat and bent his bow to take an arrow. "Whoosh" shot the rope of Xusheng's sail. The sail "Whoosh" fell into the water and the boat came across.

Zhao Yun put up a full sail on the boat and go with the wind. The flow was as fast as flying, and Xu Sheng couldn't catch up with him.

Zhou Yu exclaimed after learning that: "this man has the method of seizing heaven and earth and creating nature. He has the uncanny skill and ingenious calculation. Others are inferior to him."

5. Had Defeated Zhou Yu Thrice

After winning the battle of Chibi, Zhou Yu withdrawed Dongwu's troops and rewarded Dongwu's armed forces. However, when he heard that Liu Bei and Zhuge Liang had moved their troops to Jiangyou, he was shocked and said: "in this way, they must have the intention of taking the Southern Shire. We paid such a high price. At present, the Southern Shire is extremely easy to obtain, they have immoral intentions. If they really want South Shire, unless I'm dead." So I personally came to Jiangyou with Lu Su.

After seeing Liu Bei, Zhou Yu asked, "did you intend to occupy Southern Shire when you moved here?" As Zhuge Liang had expected, Liu Bei replied according to Zhuge Liang's plan, "if you don't occupy it, we will occupy it."

Zhou Yu said with a smile, "we, the Dongwu, have long wanted to annex the Han River. Now Southern Shire is in our hands. How can we not occupy it?"

Liu Bei said: "it's still possible. Cao Ren, who guards Southern Shire, is invincible in the world. We are afraid it's hard for you to get it."

Zhou Yu said, "if we can't occupy it down, then you can occupy it."

Liu Bei said: "Lu Su and Zhuge Liang are also here. They can be witnesses. Don't go back on your word!"

Lu Su was hesitant, but Zhou Yu had already replied, "If I say anything, I will keep my promise."

Zhou Yu and Zhuge Liang agreed that if Zhou Yu failed to capture the South Shire that Cao Ren was defending, Liu Bei could attack again.

Zhou Yu sent his soldiers to fight against Cao Ren, but he was invited by Cao Ren to enter the urn. Zhou Yu got an arrow in his left flank and quickly withdrew to the camp. A few days later, Cao Cao's army went out of the city came to the barracks of the Dongwu to shout curses. Zhou Yu first pretended to be himself wounded, and did not send forth any troops, so that lure the enemy in deeper, and finally turned defeat into victory. Cao Cao's army was defeated and fled back. Zhou Yu pursued and killed them all the way. By five a.m., it was not far from Southern Shire.

When Zhou Yu led his army and came to the South County town, he saw the banners and pennons were flaunting in the wind, and the general shouted at him, " please don't blame us! I am Zhao Yun of Changshan. I have occupied Southern Shire under the order of Zhuge Liang, the military division."

Since the death of Mrs. Liu Bei, Liu Bei had been troubled day and night. To get rid of Liu Bei and Zhuge Liang, Zhou Yu came up with a new plan. According to Zhou Yu's plan, Sun Quan pretends to betroth his sister sun Shangxiang to Liu Bei. He wants to cheat Liu Bei to the east Wu and then killed him. Zhuge Liang saw that

it was a plan and decided to turn Zhou Yu's trick to his own use. He let Liu Bei cross the river under Zhao Yun's protection to go Dong wu marry. Who knows that Empress Dowager Wu (Sun Quan ' s mother) takes a fancy to Liu Bei, not only doesn't allow Sun Quan to kill Liu Bei but also really betroths his daughter Sun Shangxiang to him. Zhou Yu wanted Liu Bei to be separated from Zhuge Liang, Guan Yu and Zhang Fei for a long time, and he hopes to use the beauty to confuse Liu Bei and make him lose his ambition to fight for the world, but he failed again. Zhou Yu let deception with deceit made it authentic. Liu Bei and Mrs. sun got married. Zhuge Liang then used strategy to let Liu Bei returned to Jingzhou safely, and Zhou Yu was ambushed. Zhuge Liang also let his soldiers sing "Zhou Yu's clever plan is to get the world, and as a result he lost the beauty and his soldiers" to mock Zhou Yu, so that Zhou Yu's wounds burst again and spit blood.

Liu Bei borrowed nine Shires of Jingxiang from the Dongwu, trying to grow and develop their own. However, Dongwu feared that Liu Bei would pose a threat to himself when he became powerful. They repeatedly asked Liu Bei to return Jingzhou. Liu Bei and Zhuge Liang refused the request of the Dongwu on the ground that they would return Jingzhou after seizing Xichuan, But they never attacked Xichuan.

Zhou Yu was so angry, So he came up with a way to help Liu Bei capture Xichuan through Jingzhou, because he had to go through Jingxiang to capture Xichuan, but Zhou Yu actually wanted to capture Jingzhou.

Zhou Yu's warships came to Jingzhou from the river.

When they got to the bottom of the city, there was no movement. Zhou Yu ordered the sergeant to call. At this time, there was a bang, and all the soldiers in the city put up their swords and guns. Zhao Yun came out and said to Zhou Yu, "your plan has been seen through by our counselor Zhuge Liang. My master Liu Bei and Liu Zhang are all Han clan relatives. We can't break faith and seizure Xichuan."

As soon as Zhou Yu heard this, he immediately turned the horse escape, surrounded by Zhuge Liang's troops. The soldiers shouted to capture Zhou Yu alive shook a distance shock over a hundred Li. Zhou Yu His sores split and he fell from the horse. His soldiers hurry saved him on the ship. A soldier said, "Liu Bei and Zhuge Liang are drinking at the top of the mountain in front of us." Zhou Yu in a rage said "You think I can't take Xichuan, I swear I will take it," He ordered the army to be urged to move forward.

When he arrived at Bachu, Zhuge Liang had sent two generals to stop the waterway and sent a letter to Zhou Yu. Zhou Yu opened it and read: "I haven't forgotten since we parted in Chaisang County. I heard that you want to seize Xichuan. I don't think you can. The terrain of Yizhou is dangerous and it can defend itself completely. If you want your army to travel thousands of Li now, it is difficult for the gods to achieve all the effects. Cao Cao defeated in the Red Cliff war and wanted revenge at any time. Now you lead the troops on an expedition. If Cao Cao takes advantage of the emptiness and enters, won't Jiangnan turn into powder? I can't bear to watch. I'd like to tell you that I hope you can think twice."

Zhou Yu looked at it, sighed a long time, and asked people to take the paper and pen, and wrote to Wuhou Sun Quan.

He said to the generals around him, "It's not that I don't want to be loyal to my country, but God wants me to die. You try your best to help Wuhou and accomplish our great cause. " Then he fainted.

When Zhou Yu woke up again, he raised his head to the sky and sighed: "Since there is Zhuge Liang in the world, why shall there be me?" He shouted several times in a row died when the age of 36.

6. Arranged Stone Fortress Cleverly

In the 18th year of Jian'an (213 AD), Zhuge Liang stayed Guan Yu to guard Jingzhou and led Zhang Fei and Zhao Yun to occupy Badong and other counties. The next year, Liu Zhang surrendered, and Liu Bei entered Chengdu and occupied Yizhou (now Sichuan) Liu Bei went out to fight and Zhuge Liang guarded Chengdu.

In March of the 22nd year of Jian'an (217 AD), Sun Quan descended to Cao. Liu Bei entered Hanzhong and won Hanzhong in the 24th year of Jian'an. In October of that year, Guan Yu was attacked and killed by general Lu Meng of Sun Quan, who lost Jingzhou.

In April 221 AD, Liu Bei ascends to the throne. Liu Chan, the son of Liu, was appointed prince. Zhuge Liang, the prime minister, designated that year as the first year of Zhangwu. In June of that year, Zhang Fei was killed by his men. In June of the second year, Liu Bei refused to listen to Zhuge Liang's words, which led to Lu Xun, the governor of the Dongwu Dynasty, breaking the Shu army in Yiling and other places, and Liu Bei retreated to the city of Baidi (now east of Fengjie, Sichuan)

After Liu Bei's defeat, Lu Xun led the victorious soldiers in the West and pursued them all the way to Kui Checkpoint. Lu Xun immediately saw the mountains and rivers in front of him, and a burst of murderous spirit rose to the sky. He reminded the generals that there ought to be ambushed in front of them and that they did not enter lightly. He ordered them to go back more than ten Li. Lu Xun ordered the soldiers to check carefully. When they came back, they reported that there was no ambush in front of them. It's true that there's not a person or a horse. They only reported that there were 80 to 90 piles of stone by the river.

Confused, Lu Xun ordered to ask the local aborigines. Soon, a few people came. Lu Xun asked, "who is the one who piled those rocks here? Why will murderous sky in the middle of the rubble pile?"

The native said, "this place is called Yubeipu. When Zhuge Liang entered Sichuan, he sent his troops here and formed an array of stones. Since then, there's always a gas-like a cloud here rising from the middle."

After hearing this, Lu Xun took a dozen people to see Stonehenge. Immediately on the hillside, he saw that there were households in all directions. Lu Xun said with a smile, "it's just a trick to confuse people. What's the use?" So he took some of them down the mountain and went into the stone formation to watch.

Lu Xun's Ministry said, "it's getting dark. Let's go home early."

When Lu Xun out of the fortress, suddenly there's a strong wind. In a flash, sand and rocks were flying, covering the sky and the earth. He saw the craggy rocks, the sand and the earth, and the sound of the river surged.

Lu Xun was shocked and said, "it's Zhuge Liang's stratagem!" When he was in a hurry want to return, he had no way to go.

The stone fortress of Wuhou invented by Zhuge Liang took the four places of heaven and earth as the main array of heaven and earth.

The northwest is the heavenly array, the southwest is the earth's array, the southeast is the wind array, and the northeast is the cloud array. Water, fire, gold and wood are used as the four kinds of strange arrays of dragon, tiger, bird and snake, as the strange soldiers.

The array is made up of green dragon on the left, white tiger on the right, Zhuque bird in the front and Yuanwu snake in the back. The general of the virtual army lives there. The stone fortress is also distributed in the general array, which is

composed of the total array is eight by eight equal to sixty-four formations and 24 formations array of rangers.

The total array consists of 32 arrays of yin and Yang, 24 arrays of Yang and 24 arrays of Yin. After the 60th array, all the soldiers who march, joined the battle, set up doubts, made up for the shortage and support, all done by scattered soldiers.

The stone fortress are extremely powerful. There are arrays in the array and teams in the team. The front can be changed into the back, the back also can be changed in the front. The forward and backward can't be fast. There are four heads eight tails.

When the enemy rushes into it, both ends can not rescue, and there is no reason for the two sides to follow each other's path; they are corresponding at the beginning and the end, which is unpredictable; foretell things accurately; act according to circumstances. Eight array method, in a burst, two array match.

They can battle or defenses. They are strong and soft. They are both illusory and real. Distinguish between host, guest, front and back. Their longitudes and latitudes change. Positive is the base, negative is the beam-column. They interact with each other for many reasons.

Lu Xun was in doubt when he saw an elderly man appear in front of the horse and said with a smile, "does the general want to get out of this battle? "

Lu Xun said, "please take us out."

The old man walked slowly on crutches and walked straight out of the Stonehenge. He didn't encounter any obstacles and went to the hillside. Lu Xun asked, "who is the old man, please?"

The old man replied, "I am Huang Chengyan, Zhuge Liang's father-in-law. As early as when my son-in-law entered Sichuan, he led the soldiers to this place and arranged the array on the beach with stones. Since then, there had always been a cloud like air flowed rising from the inside of the array. This array is called a " stone fortress chart" (also known as "eight array chart"), which consists of eight formations: sky, earth, wind, cloud, dragon, tiger, bird and snake. According to rest, survival, injury, elimination, scenery, death, panic, open eight array cycles, every hour of every day is changing, which is worth a hundred thousand elite soldiers. When him before leaving, he told me, 'if there is a general of Dongwu who is trapped in the battle, don't bring him out.' I saw the general enter from the dead gate on the mountain just now. I think you don't know this array, and you will be trapped in it. I do good deeds all my life. I can't bear to see that the general is trapped here, so I'm here to lead you out Stonehenge."

"Have you ever learned this array?" Lu asked.

"This matrix method is changed endlessly, no way to learn." said Huang.

Lu Xun hurriedly got off his horse to thank him and went back.

7. Seized Meng Huo Seven Times

In the third year of Zhangwu (223 A.D.) on April 24, Liu Bei, the front-master, died in the Baidi city because of illness. At that time, he was 63 years old. On his deathbed, Liu Bei entrusted Liu Chan, the crown prince, to Zhuge Liang. Liu Chan ascended the throne, became the post-master, reign title was Jianxing. Later, Zhuge Liang was granted the title of Marquis of Wuxiang and the governor of Yizhou. Zhuge Liang sent Deng Zhi to Soochow to restore friendship with them.

In 225 AD, Zhuge Liang, the Prime Minister of the Shu Dynasty, led the army to the south in order to consolidate the rear area. When the army was ready to withdraw, Meng Huo, the leader of the southern Yi nationality, gathered the defeated private soldiers to attack the Shu army.

Zhuge Liang learned that Meng Huo not only fought bravely, had a strong will, but also was loyal to others. He was very popular among the Yi people. Even among the Han people, many admired him, so Zhuge Liang decided to strive for Meng Huo.

Although Meng Huo was brave, he was not good at using soldiers. The first time he went to the battle, when he saw the defeat and retreat of the Shu army, he thought that the Shu army could not win himself, so he was desperate to catch up, the results he broke into the ambush circle of the Shu army and was captured.

Meng Huo believed that he was going to be executed by Zhuge Liang, so he said to himself that he would die like a hero and not lose face. Unexpectedly, Zhuge Liang himself untied him and advised him to surrender.

Meng Huo refused the surrender arrogantly. Zhuge Liang did not force him but accompanied him to watch the barracks that had already been arranged, and then specifically asked him, "how do you like the arrangement of the barracks?".

Meng Huo watched carefully. He found that the barracks were full of old, weak and disabled soldiers. He said bluntly, "I didn't know what you were, so I am defeated. Now I looked at your barracks. If it's like this, it's not difficult to win.".

Zhuge Liang didn't explain either. He smiled and let Meng Huo went back. He predicted that Meng Huo would come to steal the camp tonight, and arranged the ambush immediately.

When Meng Huo went back, he was elated to say that all the soldiers in Shu were old and weak, and he already saw the layout of the barracks clearly. There was nothing remarkable about it. If we sneak attack their barracks at three a.m. tonight, we would catch Zhuge Liang.

That night, 500 soldiers selected by Meng Huo to quietly touch the Shu army camp, without any obstruction. Meng Huo was secretly happy and thought that success was imminent. Unexpectedly, all the ambush soldiers of the Shu army came out, and Meng Huo was captured again.

Meng Huo was captured one time after another, and he dared not act recklessly anymore. He led all the soldiers back to the South Bank of Lu River, only defending but not attacking. When Shu soldiers arrived at Lu River, they could not cross the river without boats. The weather was hot and there were many difficulties.

Zhuge Liang ordered to build some rafts and bamboo rafts and sent a small number of soldiers to pretend to cross the river, but when they came to the middle of the river, as long as they meet the arrow on the other bank, they returned immediately and then went to cross the river again. On the one hand, he divided the army into two routes, around the narrow areas of the upper and lower reaches, and crossed the river to encircle the upper city where Meng Huo was defended. Later, Meng Huo was caught again.

Although Meng Huo was captured for the third time, he was still unconvinced. Zhuge Liang still didn't kill him; After entertaining him, he let him went back.

Some of the generals did not understand Zhuge Liang's practice and think he was too kind and lenient to Meng Huo. Zhuge Liang explained to everyone, "if our army wants to completely pacify the south, we must reuse people like Meng Huo. If he can sincerely contact the southerners to serve the court, he will be worth a hundred thousand troops. You're working harder now. You don't need to fight here again in the future."

After Meng Huo was captured and released this time, he made up his mind to stop fighting with Shu soldiers. But over time, the food in the barracks soon was about running out. He sent someone to borrow grain from Zhuge Liang. Zhuge Liang agreed, but asked Meng Hu to fight one‑on‑ one with the generals of the Shu army .

Meng Huo defeated several Shu generals one after another, but when he had just walked up to the side of a pile of grain, he was tripped and caught. A Shu general immediately convey Zhuge Liang's order to let Meng Huo went back and moved the grain away.

In this case, Meng Huo finally admired Zhuge Liang from his heart. In order to let all tribes pay allegiance to the kingdom of Shu, he invited the leaders of all tribes and took them to battle with the army of Shu together. As a result were led into the ambush circle by Shu soldiers, all of whom were captured.

There was a word coming from the Shu camp that let Meng Huo and others go back. Many tribal leaders jointly elected Meng Huo as the supreme leader. Meng Huo said with tears, "I have never heard of six times put back and seven catches in battle. Zhuge prime minister is so kind to us that I have no face to go back."

In this way, Zhuge Liang captured and controlled Meng Huo, the seignior of the Southern man, so that he was convinced. Meng Huo finally obeyed the Shu Han Dynasty, obey the jurisdiction of Shu Han, and proposed not to leave one soldier or one person. In November, Zhuge Liang returned to China, and Meng Huo led the cave masters, chiefs and tribal people saw off after the worship. The South was pacified and Zhuge Liang led the army back triumphantly.

8. The Empty City Stratagem

In the spring of the sixth year of Jianxing (228 A.D.), Zhuge Liang led a large army out of Qishan (in the northwest of Hexian County, Gansu Province today), and Ma Su was the pioneer warlord.

Since Zhuge Liang sent troops, Repeated get the victory, the heart was very happy. One day, he was in a meeting in the western city of Qishan (now Kangbei, Xi'an, Shaanxi Province) to discuss some matter. Suddenly a soldier reported that Cao Rui, the emperor of the state of Wei, had ordered Sima Yi to resume his official post,

and that the Wei army was about to march westward. Zhuge Liang was shocked and said, "the man I'm worried about happens to be Sima Yi."

Because Ma Su did not listen to persuasion, the strategic Street Pavilion was lost. Zhuge Liang sighed: "The whole scheme has gone to naught It's all my fault for employing people improperly!" So he gave a secret order to teach the army to pack up secretly for the purpose of returning to Hanzhong. He also sent his confidants to report to the officers, soldiers and civilians of Tianshui, Nan'an and ending counties, all of whom withdrew into Hanzhong.

Zhuge Liang's allocation had been set. All of a sudden, the soldiers came to report a dozen times in a row: "Sima Yi led 150,000 troops and swarmed to the west city!" At this time, Zhuge Liang had no even a military general, just a group of civil servants, and Simply no way to be at war with another party. Half of his 5,000 soldiers have sent to transport food and grass, leaving only 2,500 in the city.

When the officials heard the news that Sima Yi had brought his troops, they were all shocked. When Zhuge Liang ascended the city and looked out, it was dusty. The Wei army divided into two groups and came to West City. Zhuge Liang issued an order to teach "hide all the flags. If there were any soldiers who went in and out or spoke loudly, they should be beheaded immediately. Open the four gates, each with

20 soldiers, pretending to be the people, sweeping the streets. When Wei Bing arrived, he was not allowed to act without permission. I had my own plan. " Zhuge Liang was still dressed in a crane cloak and wear a silk scarf. He led two children with a guqin to sit in front of the watchtower in the city, burning incense and holding the strings.

When Sima Yi's front army came to the city, they all dared not enter the city, so they hurriedly reported to Sima Yi. After hearing this, Sima Yi said with a smile, "how can this be possible?" So he ordered the troops to stop and ride to watch. Not far from the city, he did see Zhuge Liang sitting upright on the watchtower, smiling, looking forward, burning incense and playing the piano safely and contentedly, with a calm attitude and a steady sound. On the left stood a boy with a sword in his hand, and on the right stood a boy with whisk dust in his hand. Inside and outside the city gate, about 20 people were sprinkling water and sweeping the floor with their heads down, not look around. Sima Yi was still, listening quietly. All of a sudden, his face changed and he looked nervous. He came to the middle of his Wei army and made the rear army act as the front army and the front army act as the back army. They retreated to the north mountain.

Sima Zhao, the son of Sima Yi, said: "maybe Zhuge Liang has no army in the city, pretend that this attitude. Why did you retreat?"

Sima Yi said: "Zhuge Liang is cautious all his life and never takes any risks. Today when the gate is opened wide, there will be ambushed. If our army goes in, It's going to fall into their trap. So we retreated quickly. What do you know?"

Zhuge Liang in the West City, seeing Sima Yi's troops retreating in a hurry, saw Wei's army going far away, took a long breath, wiped the cold sweat on his forehead with his hand, and laughed.

Zhuge Liang laughed. All the officials were shocked and asked Zhuge Liang, "Sima Yi is a famous general of the state of Wei. Today, he commands 150,000 elite soldiers to come here. As soon as they saw the prime minister, they turned around and left. Why is that?"

Zhuge Liang said: "he knows that I am cautious all my life and never take risks. But today, in such a big way, there must be ambush in the city, so he retreated. It's not that I'm taking risks, it's that I have to. He must have taken his army to the North Moutain path, where I have commanded Guan Xing and Zhang Bao two generals to wait for them there."

After hearing this, they all marveled and exclaimed: "the prime minister's ingenious strategy is unpredictable. If it is up to us, we shall have abandoned the city."

Zhuge Liang said, "we have only 2,500 soldiers here. If we leave the city, we will not be able to go far, and Sima Yi will surely catch us." Then he clapped his hands and laughed, saying, "if I am Sima Yi, I will not retreat." Then he ordered the people of Xicheng to move to Hanzhong with the army, "Sima Yi will come again." He said.

So Zhuge Liang left Xicheng and went to Hanzhong.

When Sima Yi learned of the plot, he sighed and praised: "I'm not as good as Zhuge Liang!"

Chapter 3 - The Controversy of His Seclusion

Chen Shou's biography of Zhuge Liang in the history of the Three Kingdoms in the Western Jin Dynasty: "Zhuge Liang became an orphan when he was very young. His uncle Zhuge Xuan was appointed as an officer of Yuzhang by Yuan Shu. His uncle Zhuge Xuan took Zhuge Liang and his younger brother Zhuge Jun go to the office." It is recorded that Zhuge Liang's father died early, and he left his hometown in Shandong with his uncle Zhuge Xuan as a refugee since childhood. Zhuge Xuan was appointed as the chief of Yuzhang (today's Nanchang area in Jiangxi Province), and

Zhuge Liang's cottage in
Xiangyang ancient Longzhong

then Zhuge Xuan took Zhuge Liang and his younger brother Zhuge to Jiangxi. "In the middle, the Imperial court appointed Zhu Hao to replace Zhuge Xuan. Zhugexuan was a friend of Liu Biao, the governor of Jingzhou, so he went to Jingzhou. After Zhuge Xuan died, Zhuge Liang went to farm. " It means that Zhuge Xuan had an official position at the level of an officer (governing Nanchang). He had no worries about food and clothing. Whoever knew that Yuan Shu was the emperor and fought against the Han Dynasty, the officials appointed by Yuan Shu naturally didn't count. So the court chosed Zhu Hao to replace Zhugexuan. "Zhugexuan was a friend of Liu Biao, the governor of Jingzhou, so he went to Jingzhou." The key point was that governer of Jingzhou Liu Biao with Zhuge Xuan were "iron brothers". At that time, the state government of Jingzhou was in Xiangyang City and "went to depend on him". Zhuge Xuan and Zhuge Liang brothers went to Xiangyang to depend on Liu Biao.

Chen Shou's father was once an officer of the Shu army under Zhuge Liang's command, while Chen Shou himself served as a Langguan under Jiang Wei. There was no doubt about the authenticity and authority of his account of Zhuge Liang's family affairs.

The book Shu Record written by Wang Yin of the Western Jin Dynasty: "In the middle of Yongxing in Jin Dynasty, General Liu Hong of Zhennan came to Longzhong, visited Zhuge Liang's former residence, erected a monument to commend him, and ordered Li Xing, the Taifu, to write: 'The emperor arranged me to listen to the sound of military drums on the north bank of Mian Water to meditate, appreciate the moral demeanor left by my ancestors, climb up to Longzhong mountain and look far away, and pay homage to Prime Minister Zhuge in his hometown.'"

It records the historical event that Liu Hong, the general of Zhennan, visited Zhuge Liang's house in Longzhong in 304 AD at the order of emperor Hui of Jin Dynasty, only 70 years after Zhuge Liang's death.

The History of Han and Jin Dynasties by Xi Zaochi in the Eastern Jin Dynasty: " Liang's family is located in Deng County of Nanyang, twenty Li west of Xiangyang City, and its name is Longzhong." Zhuge Liang's home was in a place called Longzhong under the jurisdiction of Deng County, Nanyang County at that time, twenty Li to the west of Xiangyang City. Deng County site was six kilometers northwest of Fancheng District, Xiangyang.

The Inscription of Zhuge Wuhou 's Residence by Xi Zaochi in Eastern Jin Dynasty. This is written after Xi chiseled teeth went to Longzhong in the west of Xiangyang City to pay homage to Zhuge Liang's former residence. It recorded the scene of Zhuge Liang's old house, which is decorated very beautifully by later generations. It also discusses Zhuge Liang's achievements in rejuvenating the Han Dynasty, pursuing unity, praising Zhuge Liang for his impartiality, strict law enforcement, and his contribution to the country and the people. In the temple of Wuhou Temple in Chengdu, modern Zhong Han wrote such a couplet: "The person we have worshipped together for thousands of years was Zhuge Liang; his different generations know each other was Xi Zaochi."

The Story of Jingzhou by Sheng Hongzhi in the Southern Dynasty Song: "Ten Li in the northwest of Xiangyang, named Longzhong, has Zhuge Liang house."

備曰今天下分裂日尋干戈事會之來豈有終極乎若能應之於後者則此未足爲恨也 三國志注六 入三十二

先主見諸葛亮於隆中亮家於南陽之鄧縣在襄陽城西二十里號曰隆中 三國志注 三十五

建安十三年操征劉表卒子琮迎降魏武平荊州分南郡枝江以西爲臨江郡 宋州郡志三 引習鑿齒曰

先主走將保江陵操追之 王威說劉琮曰曹操得將軍既降劉豫州已走必懈弛無備輕行單進若給威奇兵數千徼之於險操可獲也獲操則威震天下坐而虎步中夏雖廣可傳檄而定非徒收一勝之功保守今日而已此難遇之機不可失也琮不納 三國志太

廣雅書局栞

Dynasty, pursuing unity, praising Zhuge Liang for his impartiality, strict law enforcement, and his contribution to the country and the people. In the temple of Wuhou Temple in Chengdu, modern Zhong Han wrote such a couplet: "The person we have worshipped together for thousands of years was Zhuge Liang; his different generations know each other was Xi Zaochi."

The Story of Jingzhou by Sheng Hongzhi in the Southern Dynasty Song: "Ten Li in the northwest of Xiangyang, named Longzhong, has Zhuge Liang house."

The Story of South Yongzhou by Bao Zhi in Southern Dynasties Liang: "there is an old well in Zhuge Liang's former residence in Longzhong, which is now dry up."

Notes on water classics by Li Daoyuan in the Northern Dynasty: "Mian River flows

eastward to the north of Le mountain. In the past, Zhuge Liang liked to recite the song "Liang Fu Yin" and often climbed this mountain. Therefore, The folk songs usually include the name of Le mountain. Mian River flows eastward through Longzhong and north of Zhuge Liang ' s former residence. Zhuge Liang said to the later emperors of Shu, "the former Emperor visited me in Longzhong cottage Thrice and asked me about current affairs" happened here.

Jin Book / Xi Zaochi biography by Fang Xuanling in Tang Dynasty: "Huanwen's younger brother is also talented, and has many contacts with Xi Zaochi. Xi Zaochi said to his secretary: 'I went to Xiangyang on May 3 last year, and I have many feelings, which can not be expressed in words. Every time I visit my uncle, I enter from the north gate, look to the west at Longzhong, think of Zhuge Liang's recitation; look to the east at white sand, think of the voice of Phoenix.'"

The story of Xiang Mian by Wu Congzhen in the Tang Dynasty: "In the middle of Jin Yongxing, Liu Hong, Zhennan general and governor of Xiangyang, came to Longzhong, visited Zhuge Liang's former residence and erected a monument to commend him."

Carving the Tomb of Wuhou by Sun Qiao in Tang Dynasty: "Zhuge Liang was an ancient great sage. Try to do something which is known as impossible, because Liu Bei entrusted him with the world in Longzhong, which made Zhuge Liang willing to abandon his comfortable life.

Art and Literature Collection, Volume 7 by Ouyang Xun in Tang Dynasty: Seven Li in west of Dengcheng, there is Le Mountain. Zhuge Liang often climbed this mountain and recite Liang Fu Yin."

Introduction of Memorial Before Departure by Li Shan in Tang Dynasty: "it is noted that Zhuge Liang lived in Deng County of Nanyang in the Spring and Autumn

Period of Han and Jin Dynasties. Jingzhou map said that there was Zhuge Liang's house in the southwest of the old county of Dengcheng, that's where Liu Bei visited Zhuge Liang Thrice."

History as a Mirror, Volume 65 by Sima Guang in the Northern Song Dynasty: " Zhuge Liang lived in Xiangyang Longzhong in seclusion. He often compared himself with Guan Zhong and Yue Yi."

The Story of the Peace Earth by Yue Shi in the Northern Song Dynasty (Xiangzhou, the 4th East of Shannan Road): "The former residence of Zhuge Liang in Xiangyang, according to the records of Shu, is where Liu Bei's three visits to Zhuge Liang took place. There is a well, 13 meters deep and 1.6 meters wide, well preserved."

Poetry notes in the valley by Huang Tingjian in the Northern Song Dynasty: "in Longzhong, according to the records of the later Han Dynasty, Nanyang belongs to Jingzhou."

The prime tortoise of the record bureau by Wang Qinruo in the Northern Song Dynasty: "Zhuge Liang, style name Zhuge Liang, Langya Yangdu people. His uncle Zhuge Xuan with Liubiao of Jingzhou was old friends , so they went to join Liu Biao. After Zhuge Xuan died, Zhuge Liang lived in Longzhong, Deng County, Nanyang. Zhuge Liang often compares himself with Guan Zhong and Yue Yi. Liu Bei visited Zhuge Liang in Longzhong Thrice. Zhuge Liang was farming in Longzhong, he was 2.5 meters tall."

Memorial to the Temple of Wuhou of Zhuge by Li Shi in the Southern Song Dynasty: Our life is difficult and born in wrong time. I would like to visit Longzhong in person and pay homage to Zhuge Liang's virtue, but I can't."

Biography of Zhuge Liang by Zheng Qiao in the Southern Song Dynasty: "After the death of zhugexuan, Zhuge Liang's home was in Deng County, Nanyang, more than 20 Li west of Xiangyang City, named Longzhong. Zhuge Liang, who was farming there, liked to recite Liang Fu Yin."

Biography of the prime minister Zhuge Liang of the Han Dynasty by Zhang Shi in the Southern Song Dynasty: "Zhuge Liang's style name was Zhuge Liang, a native of Langya Yangdu. He became an orphan when he was very young. He followed his uncle Zhuge Xuan and attached himself to Liu Biao of Jingzhou. After Zhuge Xuan died, he moved to Longzhong, Nanyang."

Ode to the Dragon Temple by Liu Guangzu in Southern Song Dynasty: "Zhuge Liang is a sleeping dragon. He used to farm in Longzhong, Nanyang. He compared himself with Guan Zhong and Yue Yi."

Public opinion landscape by Wang Xiangzhi in the Southern Song Dynasty: " According to the Story of Jingzhou, there was a well in Zhuge Liang's former residence. According to the County Annals of Yuanhe, Wan Mountain is 21 Li west of Xiang yang, which is the boundary between Wan Mountain and Deng County of Nanyang County. According to the historical records of Han and Jin Dynasties, Zhuge Liang's

family is located 20 Li west of Xiangyang City, named Longzhong. Zhuge Liang said that Liu Bei, the former Emperor, visited me thrice in the cottage, that is, he went in and out of the Thrice Gate of Xiangyang mansion."

The story of Chaozhen temple in Chengdu by Wei Liaoweng in the Southern Song Dynasty: "The result of my research was, Zhuge Liang's former residence was in Longzhong."

Memorial article for Zhuge Liang by Zheng Ruqiao in the Southern Song Dynasty: " Zhuge Liang was born in the late Han Dynasty. He studied in Longzhong. He was loyal, righteous, clever and did not seek fame."

Zhuangjing collection by Li Junmin in the Jin Dynasty: "It is said that Xiangyang Shuixi Gate is the Thrice Visit Gate. Liu Bei, the former Emperor, went to Longzhong to see Zhuge Liang. Zhuge Liang's former residence was 20 Li west of Xiangyang City."

Unification of the great Yuan Dynasty in Yuan Dynasty: "in the Spring and Autumn Period of Han and Jin Dynasties, Zhuge Liang lived in Nanyang, 20 Li west of Xiangyang, named Longzhong. Gejing, on Xiangyang Road. In Jingzhou, there are wells in Zhuge Liang's house. Sangu gate, in Xiangyang Road, Zhuge Liangyun, Sangu minister in the grass, since then also out of the gate."

The grand collection of clans in the Yuan Dynasty: "Zhuge Liang, with a clear character. Living in Longzhong, Nanyang. In Jian'an of the Han Dynasty, Xu Shu was named Liu Bei, who said Zhuge Zhuge Liang was also named Wolong. Prepare for thrice in the grass, light is up."

A general guide to a historical compilation by Hu Yigui of Yuan Dynasty: "(Liu Bei) saw Zhuge Liang in Longzhong. According to Zhuge Liang's agreement in Longzhong, Wu can help but not plan.

Unification of Ming Dynasty, Xiangyang mansion, mountains article in Ming Dynasty: Longzhong mountain, 25 Li northwest of the Fucheng, under the Longzhong academy, Han Zhuge Liang taste hidden here. Zhuge Liang's house is located in the middle of the mountain, 22 Li west of the mansion, where Zhuge Liang of Shu Han lived. There is a summer resort in the west of the house. Because Liu Bei paid three visits to Zhuge Liang's cottage in Longzhong, there were the Gate of Thrice Visit there."

Dengzhou Chronicles of Jiajing in the Ming Dynasty: "In the past 12 years, Liu Bei visited Zhuge Liang in Longzhong thrice. Xu Shu sees Liu Bei in Xinye, and Liu Bei values him. Xu Shu recommended Zhuge Liang. Zhuge Liang's home is in Deng County, Nanyang Shire. Its name was Longzhong."

Memorials of famous officials in successive dynasties by Huang Huai and Yang Shiqi in the Ming Dynasty: "Zhuge Liang worked hard in Longzhong. A wild old man in Zhuge Liang's Longzhong met the first lord. In the twelfth year of Dinghai, the year of zhaolie saw Zhuge Liang in Longzhong, the twenty seventh year of that time. The later master Zen was born in Jingzhou. In the third year of Zhangwu, guimao crown prince Chan took the throne. In the 17th year of Zhangwu's reign, he was born in the year of Dinghai."

Complete biography of Zhuge Liang by Yang Shiwei in the Ming Dynasty: "in the 12th year of Dinghai, in the 27th year of the Ming Dynasty, he saw Zhuge Liang in Longzhong. In the Spring and Autumn Period of the Han and Jin Dynasties, Liang's family lived in Deng County of Nanyang, 20 Li west of Xiangyang, and its name was Longzhong."

The book of Zhuge Zhong and Wuhou by Wang Shiqi of Ming Dynasty: "Liu Bei saw Zhuge Liang in Longzhong. A world dragon is like a Zhuge Liang one, square and high lying in the middle of the lung, holding the knee for a long time."

Official collection by Feng Qi of the Ming Dynasty: "Zhuge Liang of Langxie lives in Longzhong of Xiangyang. When he compares himself with Guan Zhong, he is not allowed to be a man. Liu Bei saw Zhuge Liang in Longzhong."

The story of Guangyu by Lu Yingyang in the Ming Dynasty: "Zhuge Liang lived in seclusion in Longzhong mountain and under the north of Fucheng. Zhuge Liang's house has three gates at the foot of Longzhong mountain."

Sequel to the chronicle of events by Wang Wei of the Ming Dynasty: "Liu Bei, Zhuge Liang, a scholar in charge of social affairs, is a year old. Liang family in The Spring and Autumn Period of Han and Jin Dynasties is located in Deng County, Nanyang

City, 20 Li in Xiangyang City. Its name is Longzhong."

Records of loyalty and righteousness by Wang Ming of the Ming Dynasty: "Zhuge Liang, a Zhuge Liang character, was born in Langya and lived in Longzhong, Xiangyang. Liu Bei saw it, and Liang came out."

Records of the Great Qing Dynasty unification, Xiangyang mansion, Historical Site article in Qing Dynasty: "Zhuge Liang house, in Xiangyang County, in the middle of the Shandong. According to the water Scripture, in the northern part of Zhuge Liang's old house in Mianyang, Liu Chan, in a bright language, said, "the first emperor, the third adviser, was in the thatched cottage, and the adviser was in charge of the current affairs, that is, this house... Zhugeliang's family is in Longzhong mountain of Deng County, twenty miles west of Xiangyang City. County records: thatched cottage is on the side of the mountain, half of it is knee cradling stone, which can seat more than ten people like a mound, and below are farmlands."

Xinye county annals of Qianlong in the Qing Dynasty: "Zhuge Liang is Zhuge Liang, born in Langya, living in Longzhong, Xiangyang. In the 12th year of Jian'an (Liu Bei), Zhuge Liang and Zhuge Liang went to Longzhong."

Reading the summary of history Fang Yu Xiangyang County by Gu Zuyu in the Qing Dynasty: " Longzhong mountain, twenty-five Li northwest of Xiangyang Prefecture, where the Wuhou of Zhuge lived. First, he led the Xuzhou herdsmen and was defeated by Yuan Shu, Lu Bu and Cao Cao. Then, he built a new field according to Liu Biao and thrice considered Zhuge Liang in Longzhong."

Biography of Zhuge Liang by Wang Fuli in Qing Dynasty: "After Zhuge Xuan, Zhuge Liang's uncle, died, Zhuge Liang planted land in Longzhong and liked to recite Liang Fu Yin. Zhuge Liang's home is 20 Li west of Xiangyang, Deng County, Nanyang Shire, named Longzhong (now Xiangyang mansion of Huguang) Xu Shu recommended Zhuge Liang to Liu Bei, and Liu Bei to Longzhong to visit Zhuge Liang."

Outline editor by Ye Yun in the Qing Dynasty: "Zhuge Liang of Langya lived in Longzhong of Xiangyang. When he compared himself with Guan Zhong and Yue Yi, he was not allowed to do so. Longzhong, the name of the mountain, was in the northwest of the Xiangyang mansion. Liu Bei saw Zhuge Liang in Longzhong."

It could be seen from the above documents that Zhuge Liang's seclusion land and plowing land were not controversial.

Chapter 4 - When did controversy start?

The present Nanyang city was called "Wancheng" from the Han Dynasty to the Three Kingdoms. According to Sima Qian's Qin History in the Western Han Dynasty, in the 35th year of the reign of King Zhaoxiang of Qin Dynasty (272 BC), Nanyang Shire was first established. According to the Hanshu written by Ban Gu in the Eastern Han Dynasty, Nanyang Shire was under the jurisdiction of 36 counties in the Western Han Dynasty, of which 33 counties were located in the northeast of Hanshui and 3 counties in the southwest of Han Water.

Atlas of Yuanhe Shire and County by Li Jifu in Tang Dynasty: "Wan Mountain is located in the eleventh mile west of Xiangyang County. At the boundary with Deng County of Nanyang Shire, the old saying goes: 'Xiangyang has no West', which means that the west of Xiangyang is close to the border."

That was to say, although Longzhong was not far from the west of Xiangyang City at that time, it was under the jurisdiction of Deng County, Nanyang Shire when it passed the Wan Mountain, which was 11 Li west of Xiangyang City. At that time

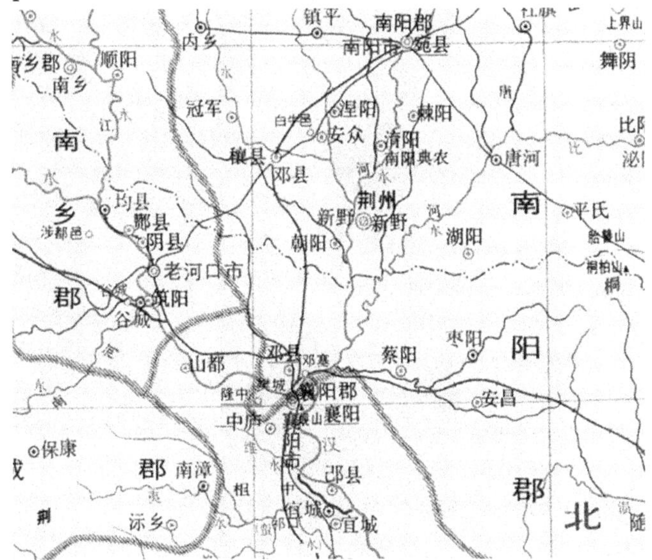

Nanyang as a shire, the scope was very large. The map of the Jingzhou History Department of the Eastern Han Dynasty in the atlas of Chinese history compiled by Tan Qixiang shows that the boundary between Nan yang Shire and Nan Shire was crisscross. The northeast part of Nan Shire was to the north of Hanshui, and the south of Nanyang Shire was to the green forest mountain. Deng County, which was subordinate to Nanyang County, had a piece to the south of Hanshui and goes deep into Xiangyang. The Eastern Han part of the atlas of Chinese history clearly indicates that Longzhong was under the jurisdiction of Deng County, Nanyang

County at that time.

The historical map of China, published by the Publishing Department of China University of culture, Taiwan, from 1980 to 1984 (sixty-nine to seventy-three years of the Republic of China), was compiled by Cheng Guangyu and Xu Shengmo, supervised by Zhang Qiyun and drawn by Cheng Anlan, Huang Banghua and Shi Huiqin. The position of Longzhong in the picture of Three Kingdoms Confrontation was exactly the same as the picture above.

Another example was the hometown of Liu Xiu, the founding emperor of the Eastern Han Dynasty. According to the book of Emperor Guangwu of the later Han Dynasty, "Emperor Guangwu taboo Xiu, style name Wenshu, Caiyang people of Nanyang, and the grandson of emperor Gaozu IX." Zhang Heng, a scientist in the Eastern Han Dynasty, called it "True dragon emperor was from White Water Village, Pine Seed Pavilion had a miracle." At that time, it belonged to Baishui village, Chongling Township, Caiyang County, Nanyang Shire, but now it belongs to White Water Village, Wudian Town, Zaoyang County, Xiangyang City.

From the Yuan Dynasty, Nanyang began to have some memorial buildings related to Zhuge Liang. Because Zhuge Liang had the words "I used to be a common man, farming in Nanyang" in "Memorial before departure", then began to have a statement that Nanyang is Zhuge Liang's seclusion in those years.

From the spring of the second year of emperor Wuzong's reign (AD 1309), Zhuge Academy was built starting in Nanyang, to the autumn of the first year of emperor Renzong's reign (AD 1312), it took more than three years.

After the completion of the Zhuge academy, Cheng Jufu of the Yuan Dynasty wrote the inscription of Zhuge Academy in Nanyang on behalf of the emperor. In the second year of

White Water Temple, Wudian, Xiangyang

Ming Yingzong's orthodoxy (1437 A.D.), a man named Kang Konggao first built the chronicles of Nanyang Prefecture, and collected the Inscription on a tablet written by Cheng Jufu in the Yuan Dynasty in volume 11 of Chronicles of Nanyang Prefecture. According to this inscription of Cheng's surname, "in the seven Li west of Nanyang City, there are rolling hills, which are called 'Wolong Hillock'. There are well, which was deep. Those who are called 'Zhuge Well' are said to be loyal to the former residence of Wuhou and worshiped by the people." It was pointed out that Wolong Hillock in Nanyang was "the former residence of Han Xiangzhong and Wuhou" and "handed down". The so-called "legend" was actually "legend". The so-called "legend" means that there was no affirmation, not to mention evidence of " truth".

In fact, from 207 when Zhuge Liang assisted Liu Bei to 1279 when Song Dynasty perished, 1,072 years was an 11 century time span. The name of "Wolong Hillock" in Nanyang was not recorded in historical documents, nor was it recorded that Wolong Hillock in Nanyang was the land where Zhuge Liang lived in seclusion or farming.

Chapter 5 - Henan Chronicles Seclusion LZ

According to many local records of Henan Province, Zhuge Liang's seclusion place was in Longzhong of Xiangyang, no doubt.

1. Dengzhou Local chronicles in Jiajing of Ming Dynasty

Dengzhou Local chronicles were compiled by Pan Tingnan, the governor of Dengzhou during the Jiajing period of the Ming Dynasty. In the second volume of the annals "county records", it was clearly mentioned that "In the twelfth year, Liu Bei according to the recommendation of Xu Shu, thrice to Nanyang Deng County, a place called Longzhong visited Zhuge Liang."

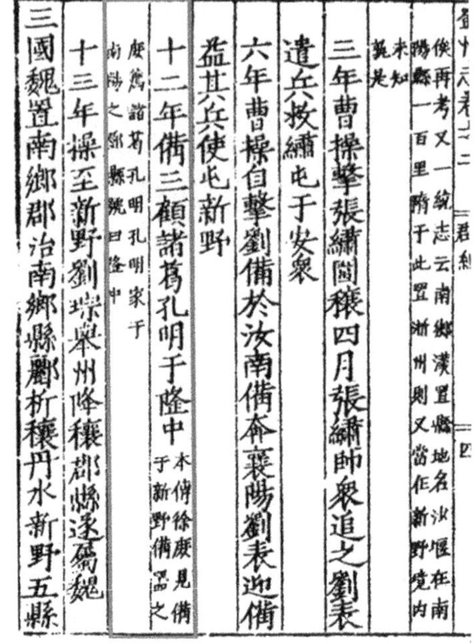

2. Records of Emperors in Deng Zhou Records

In the third volume of the annals, "emperor's history records", Liu Bei "according to the recommendation of Xu Shu, I went to Longzhong thrice to visit Zhuge Liang."

3. Notes of NY Chronicles in Jiajing of Ming Dynasty

During the period of the Republic of China, Nanyang revised the chronicles of Nanyang Prefecture in Jiajing of the Ming Dynasty and compiled it into the annotation of the chronicles of Nanyang Prefecture in Jiajing of the Ming Dynasty.

Mr. Zhang Jiamou was from Wancheng District, Nanyang city. He was an educator and librarian of the Republic of China, and served as a member of the Henan Provincial Parliament, editor of Henan Tongzhi Museum, director of Henan Provincial Museum, etc. He initiated a new school in Henan Province, and founded Nanyang Jingye school, Henan women's normal school and other schools. At that time, he and Li shican were called "North Li Nanzhang" in Henan education circle. He once strongly sponsored and personally participated in the excavation of Yin Ruins in Anyang; founded the first library in Nanyang, and donated all his books to the library; presided over and participated in the compilation of records of territory evolution, records of Nanyang Prefecture, records of Nanyang County, records of Henan Tongzhi, records of Fangcheng County, records of Gong County, records of Mengjin County, and copies of Zhongzhou poetry. He also wrote books such as Yi ware of Shire County, Yi ware of Yin Xu, Yi ware of Ji County, etc.

In the proofreading note "historic sites" on the inscription in Jiajing of the Ming Dynasty , "Zhuge Liang's reclusive in Wolong Hillock is wrong. Zhuge Liang's former Residence was located in Deng County, Nanyang Shire, twenty Li west of Xiangyang City, named Longzhong. In the Han Dynasty, Longzhong was indeed Deng County, but not Wan. In the Han Dynasty, Xiangyang was a county under the jurisdiction of Nan Shire, which was 11 Li away from the western boundary. Therefore, the water classics noted that Xiangyang had no West." The proofreading notes that it is wrong to say that "Wolong Hillock is Longzhong" Because Xiangyang Longzhong belonged to Nanyang Shire at the time of the Qin Dynasty and later did not belong to it, so Nanyang people call

照磨乾州張邦直郡庠生李君書孫慶家

案碑授襄瀋光化正奏請頒題額祭文因謂此亦隆中盖非

於南陽之邓县在襄阳城西二十里号曰隆中此汉隆中确属邓县

襄无西且侯自表臣本布衣躬耕南阳不谓襄阳也至碑谓唐宋已

又谓侯为汉漾阳人允误三国志侯传注引汉晋春秋亮家

不属宛汉时襄阳为南郡属县且县境西止十一里故水经注谓

把侯是也侯初亡所在求为立庙不听百姓遂因时节私祭之

新野縣志　卷之七　古蹟　四

昭烈皇帝建安六年帝以左將軍領豫州牧□□

敗於汝南遂奔劉表比至表郊迎之益其衆使□□

十二年操北伐烏桓帝勸表襲許表不能用是年

三顧諸葛亮於隆中情好日密有魚水之契亮爲

諸葛亮字孔明本琅琊人寓居襄陽隆中徐庶謂昭

烈曰孔明臥龍也將軍豈願見之乎帝曰君與俱

來庶曰此人可就見不可屈致也帝於是凡三顧

44

WoLong Hillock "here is also Longzhong". At the same time, the proofreading notes also admitted that Xiangyang Longzhong really belonged to Deng County of Nanyang Shire in the Han Dynasty, Xiangyang County West 11 Li was indeed the west boundary of Xiangyang County, and Xiangyang really had no West."

The proofreading note "seclusion" about " seclusion in Ye County at the end of Han Dynasty" and once again puts forward: " Zhuge Liang travels to Jingzhou to study, and often recited every morning and night. The governor of Jingzhou in the Han dynasty ruled Xiangyang, and had jurisdiction over Nanyang County. Zhuge Liang's family is located in Deng County, Nanyang Shire, 20 Li west of Xiangyang City, so Zhuge Liang claims to cultivate

> 岡臨通衢又重以侯故題詠繁富康熙中知府羅景圖而輯之為卧龍岡志今方謀續輯云按南陽有諸葛忠武侯祠始見宋忠人家集至元明皆有敕賜廟學祭品國志碑而隨名益著賞家襄陽之祠非是考三國志亮而隨名益著叔父或依謂荊侯州牧劉表是時表軍亮宅在襄陽城西為信水經注謂沔水迎亮舊宅是也然漢荊州八郡南陽居首襄陽四

> 岡臨通衢又重以侯故題詠繁富康熙中知府羅景圖而輯之為卧龍岡志今方謀續輯云按南陽有諸葛忠武侯祠始見宋忠人家集至元明皆有敕賜廟學祭品國志碑而隨名益著賞家襄陽之祠非是考三國志亮而隨名益著叔父或依謂荊侯州牧劉表是時表軍亮宅在襄陽城西為信水經注謂沔水迎亮舊宅是也然漢荊州八郡南陽居首襄陽四

Nanyang. Ye county belongs to Yingchuan county and is subordinate to Yuzhou. If Zhuge Liang lived in Yexian, he would not be called Nanyang of Jingzhou."

The proofreading note denied that Zhuge Liang lived in seclusion in Ye County at the end of Han Dynasty, and affirmed again that Zhuge Liang's family was in Deng County, Nanyang County, 20 Li west of Xiangyang City.

4. Records of Xinye County by Qianlong of Qing Dynasty

Xinye county annals compiled in the 19th year of Qianlong's reign in the Qing Dynasty was the most complete one of Xinye county's remaining old annals.

> 為鄧縣資隸南陽故侯自表謂躬耕南陽漢晉春秋亦謂亮家南陽之鄧縣在襄陽城西二十里以此推之南陽祀侯固宜之歷代迄今蔡之居以像攸之隆中並稽於以見侯德感人之深而民稱曩之好之攸同前有所因舉英敢廢況南陽於侯其名自昔為著尤非他邑比歟今考原本舊志列入流寓而附考於此

> 為鄧縣資隸南陽故侯自表謂躬耕南陽漢晉春秋亦謂亮家南陽之鄧縣在襄陽城西二十里以此推之南陽祀侯固宜之歷代迄今蔡之居以像攸之隆中並稽於以見侯德感人之深而民稱曩之好之攸同前有所因舉英敢廢況南陽於侯其名自昔為著尤非他邑比歟今考原本舊志列入流寓而附考於此

The annals volume seven "historic sites" said "twelve years of Jian'an Liu Bei visited Zhuge Liang in Longzhong thrice. " He also said, "Zhuge Liang was born in Langya, living in Longzhong, Xiangyang."

Xinye local Chi clearly defined Liu Bei thrice visited Zhuge Liang in today's Xiangyang Longzhong, not Nanyang Wolong Hillock.

5. The Revised Records of Nanyang County by Guangxu

Pan Shoulian, the magistrate of Nanyang County, presided over the compilation of Nanyang county annals during the reign of Guangxu in the Qing Dynasty.

The compilation team was composed of 17 eminent Confucians, such as the four Jinshi, the six Juren and the seven Xiucai, who were well-known in Nanyang literary and political circles at that time. Through five county directors, it lasted six years, and its manuscript was published in Guangxu 30 years. Because of its high compilation quality, it was later included in the summary of the renewal of Siku Quanshu.

The new Nanyang county annals in Guangxu of the Qing Dynasty introduces the Wuhou Temple of Zhugezhong in Wolong Hillock: "Zhuge Liang's family was in Xiangyang, and the temple of Nanyang was not right. At that time the army of Liu Biao was in Xiangyang, the Former Residence of Zhuge Liang was in Longzhong. Shuijingzhu record Mian River pass the former Residence of Zhuge Liang."

He added: "However, In the Han Dynasty, Nanyang was the first of the Eight Shire in Jingzhou, and Deng county was subordinate to Nanyang. Therefore, Zhuge Liang claimed to "farming in Nanyang". According to the History of Han and Jin Dynasties, Zhuge Liang's home is in Deng County of Nanyang, and 20 Li west in Xiangyang City. Based on this, Nanyang imitates Zhuge Liang's architecture. It shows Zhuge Liang's deep moral character and moving people, the People from all directions held a memorial service. This is the note to the original records."

It said very clearly, although "building the same house, like Longzhong's, shows Zhuge Liang's deeply moving virtue, and the spontaneous mourning of the people." That is to say, only to satisfy the people's love for Zhuge Liang, Nanyang Wolong Hillock "built a house to look like it". That is to say, Nanyang Wolong Hillock is just imitating Xiangyang Longzhong.

Chapter 6 - Seclusion Place is in Longzhong

1. Biography of Zhuge Liang

In 1976, the biography of Zhuge Liang compiled by the Propaganda Department of Nanyang Municipal Party committee, published by Henan people's publishing house, printed by Nanyang regional printing factory, and issued by Henan Xinhua bookstore. Unified Book No. 11105. 7, price 0.18 yuan. There are 82 pages in the book. In Zhuge Liang's biography, it is believed that Nanyang Wolong Hillock was a memorial place and Xiangyang Longzhong was place of seclusion.

Longzhong, 20 Li northwest of Xiangyang, was under the jurisdiction of Deng County, Nanyang Shire. Nanyang Shire was located in the throat of Hubei, Henan and other places, with developed transportation, In the late Eastern Han Dynasty, there were seven Shires in Jingzhou (including Nanyang, Southern Shire, Jiangxia, Wuling, Guiyang, Lingling and Changsha) In the Han Dynasty, it was also the largest Shire in the Jingzhou, governing 37 cities, more than 528, 500 households and more than 243, 000 people. Longzhong has beautiful mountains and clear waters. The famous Han River flows slowly from the north to the east of Zhuge Liang's former residence. Around the hut was a pine forest and a bamboo forest.

诸葛亮十七岁的时候（公元一九七年），叔父诸葛玄去世了。这年，他便在隆中盖了几间草屋，和姐弟一起定居下来。

隆中在襄阳西北二十里，当时属南阳郡邓城管辖。南阳郡地处荆、豫咽喉，交通发达，是东汉末年荆州七郡（包括南阳郡、南郡、江夏郡、武陵郡、桂阳郡、零陵郡及长沙国。汉时国亦相当于郡）中最大的一郡，辖三十七城，五十二万八千五百多户，二百四十三万多人。隆中山青水秀，有名的汉水从诸葛亮定院北面向东南缓缓流过，草屋周围是一片苍松翠竹，诸葛亮在这里度过了十个寒暑。小小的隆中实际上成了他的第二个故乡，所以他自称"躬耕于南阳"。

隆中十年，诸葛亮曾说过"苟全性命于乱世，不求闻达于诸侯"。其实，他是认真研究历史，研究现实，密切关注当时的政局，深入思考实现中国统一的问题，以天下为怀的。

Zhuge Liang had spent ten years here. Longzhong actually became his second hometown, so he called himself "Farming in Nanyang."

2. Records of Henan Scenery

In 1985, Henan people's Publishing House published the Records of Henan Scenery. The chapter "Wuhou Temple" said: "(Zhuge Liang) lived in seclusion in Xiangyang west Longzhong." "Liu Bei, a descendant of the Han Royal Family, thrice visited the cottage in Longzhong." " Zhuge Liang therefore left Longzhong and assisted Liu Bei to attack the Central Plains." "It is known that Zhuge Liang lived in seclusion in the ancient Longzhong of Xiangyang, Hubei Province." "Zhuge Liang said in his 'Memorial Before Departure' that 'I used to be a common people who to farm in Nanyang.'" It was obvious that Nanyang Shire was not today's Nanyang city. Later generations, out of admiration, built temples in Nanyang today to offer sacrifices." The book was organized and compiled by the government of Henan Province. It had won the first prize of excellent achievements in local history records of Henan Province. This brochure had been put in every room of Nanyang hotel. Chief

武　侯　祠

武侯祠天下有三：一在湖北襄阳古隆中；一在四川成都市——"丞相祠堂何处寻，锦官城外柏森森"；另一处则坐落在南阳卧龙冈上。

诸葛亮（公元181—234年）字孔明，琅琊阳都（今山东沂水南）人。他少有俊逸之才，胸怀治国奇志。十七岁时，他跟随在江南为宦的叔父到了襄阳，后因叔父罢职，于是在襄阳西隆中结茅隐居，他躬耕垄亩，攻读史籍，关心世事，常以管仲、乐毅自比，以天下为己任。建安十二年（公元207年），汉室后裔刘备三顾茅庐于隆中，恳请他出山用世，匡扶天下。孔明遂离开隆中，佐刘备攻伐中原，后定都成都，建立蜀汉。蜀汉政权的建立，使当时天下形成了三分鼎立的局面。刘备死后，孔明佐后主刘禅，被封为武乡侯。诸葛亮用事谨慎，以致积劳成疾，建兴十二年病殁于军中。

诸葛亮身为蜀相，以身殉职，鞠躬尽瘁。据《三国志》载，当时人闻其逝，"百姓巷祭"，"戎夷野祀"，服缞遍军旅。

人们知道，湖北襄阳古隆中为孔明隐居躬耕之所，那里有武侯祠一座。襄阳秦汉时属南阳郡，诸葛亮在《出师表》中说过："臣本布衣，躬耕于南阳。"很明显，这里所说的"南阳"系南阳郡，并非今日之南阳市。后人出于仰慕，于今日南阳建祠以祀。顾嘉蘅为襄阳人，他当然以家乡有武侯胜迹而自豪，但他身为南阳太守，也还要维护地方风采。顾在任期间，重修了武侯祠。人请其题联，他一挥而就："心在朝廷，原无论先主后主；名高天

· 173 ·

48

editor Hu Shihou was from Runan, Henan Province. He used to be the consultant of Henan Social Science Association, vice president of the Chinese Ancient Opera Association, vice president of the Chinese Three Kingdoms Association, vice president of the Yellow River Culture Research Association, etc., enjoying the special allowance of the State Council. Tang Zhangping, another editor in chief, is from Yunxiao, Fujian Province. He used to be a researcher of Henan Academy of Social Sciences, deputy editor in chief and President of the academic journal of Zhongzhou, executive director of China Quyuan society, director of China Poetry Society and Secre tary- General of Henan aes thetics society. Once won the title of an expert with outstanding contribution who enjoys the special allowance of the State Council.

葛亮隐居之地的真伪，争执辨认了数百年。清代家居襄阳而在南阳做郡守的顾家衡，为评判争执，书写了一副对联，挂于大殿两边："心在朝廷原无论先主后主；名高天下何必辨襄阳南阳。"顾家衡大概觉得这种争论无谓，又官居南阳，左右为难，用了这种办法，和了个稀泥，企图了却此案。正巧，在武侯祠后殿南廊嵌有郑板桥别具一格的题字"难得糊涂"。作为顾家衡对联的横楣，再恰当不过了。其实，诸葛先生真实的隐居地是在距此一百多里的襄阳隆中。汉代襄阳，归南阳管辖。这时，我想起了一位地委领导同志和我

3. Story of Scenery in Central Plain

"In fact, Zhuge Liang's real place of seclusion was in Longzhong, Xiangyang, which is more than 100 Li away," said Story of Central Plain Scenery, published by Xinhua Publishing House in 1986 by Wang Biao, a reporter from Henan Branch of Xinhua news agency, was the author of the book, which was a result of his in -depth interviews and extensive investigated.

4. Introduction to Wuhou Temple

In 1987, " Introduction to Wuhou Temple" compiled by Nanyang Museum: "Zhuge Liang lived in seclusion in Longzhong, Nanyang (near

49

Xiangyang, Hubei Province)", "Liu Bei thrice visited the cottage in Longzhong" and "since then, he left Long zhong to assist Liu Bei". "The mausoleum at the back of Wuhou Temple in Wolong Hillock (Nanyang) is a memorial building built by later generations ac cording to Zhuge Liang's living conditions."

武 侯 祠 简 介

　　武侯祠是纪念三国时期的卓越政治家、军事家诸葛亮的祠堂（相当于纪念馆）。

　　诸葛亮（公元一八一至二三四年），字孔明，琅琊阳都（今山东沂水南）人。少年时曾随叔父诸葛玄去江西南昌，不久，因叔父的太守职务被他人代替，诸葛亮便隐居在南阳郡的隆中（今湖北襄阳附近）。献帝建安十二（公元二〇七）年，刘备"三顾茅庐"见到了诸葛亮，当时他为刘备提出连合孙权，抗拒曹操的战略方针，并建议先取得荆、益二州作基地，然后出师，北伐中原统一天下。从此他就离开隆中辅佐刘备，先后取得了荆州、益州和汉中等地，建立了蜀汉政权，形成了魏、蜀、吴三国鼎立的三分局势。刘备死后，后主刘禅封诸葛亮为武乡侯，公元二三四年秋，他病殁于军中，后世为纪念诸葛亮兴建的祠堂，也因以"武侯"命名。

　　南阳卧龙冈上的武侯祠，相传建于唐、宋年间，后遭兵焚，直到元朝大德二（公元一二九八）年，又进行重建。清康熙壬辰年再次修葺增建，才成为现在这样一个庙宇。武侯祠的主要建筑分前后两部分，前部以大拜殿为中心，左右两廊为两翼，是过去人们春秋时节祭祀诸葛亮的地方。后部的茅庐、古柏亭、野云庵、躬耕亭、伴月台等，是后人根据诸葛亮"躬耕"时的生活起居而兴建的纪念性建筑物。武侯祠山门外，又有相传为诸葛亮隐居时用过的水井和经常读书的地方——读书台。

committee. "It was recognized that the Wuhou Temple in Wolong Hillock, Nanyang, was a memorial building rather than a former residence. In the Wuhou Temple in Nanyang, ' Zhuge Lu although it was a forgery', because of Zhuge Liang's great fame, ' Nanyang Wuhou Temple is quite famous.'" In the chapter of the list of celebrities, the book introduces 26 Nanyang and ancient and modern celebrities who lived in Nanyang. Zhuge Liang is not included in it. In the

"三顾茅庐"的故事幻象皆知。诸葛亮，原也只凡人，望果长保植以给衣食，树茅庐草庵以遮风雨。通过自学和实践，才使他成为百代瞩目的政治家和军事家。他确实为国家社稷和黎民苍生干了一番事业。他死后，"所在各求为立庙。百姓遂因时节私祭于道陌上。"（《三国志》裴松之注引《襄阳记》）后，西南少数民族率先为诸葛亮建庙享祭，接着，全国陆续修建近百座武侯祠，直到今天，仍有九处。南阳的"诸葛庐"、"抱膝石"等等成蔡品。但由于诸葛亮自称"臣本布衣，躬耕于南阳"，唐人刘禹锡在他的名文《陋室铭》中曾将"南阳诸葛庐"和"西蜀子云亭"相提并论，故而南阳的武侯祠便颇有名气了。我曾去过许多处武侯祠，虽规模不一，格局各异，但殿宇亭台间都长着一蓬

5. Nanyang - -a Historical and Cultural City

In 1987, Nanyang, a His torical and Cultural City, was published by the Propaganda Department of Nanyang Municipal Party

chapter of the

famous verses, the Longzhong Countermeasure is included.

It can be seen from this that the authoritative materials of relevant parties to the dispute all admit that Longzhong, Xiangyang, Hubei Province is the place where Zhuge Liang lives in seclusion.

Chapter 7 - Reclusive Land in Longzhong

In addition to the numerous historical records from the Jin Dynasty to the Yuan Dynasty, Zhuge Liang's relatives and friends whole were in Xiangyang and nearby. Zhuge Xuan, Zhuge Liang's uncle, and Liu Biao, Jingzhou mu (governing Xiangyang) were old friends. Zhuge Liang's eldest sister married Kuai Qi of the Kuai family of Zhonglu County (now Nanzhang County, Hubei province), and the second elder sister married Pang Shanmin, the son of Pang Degong of Xiangyang. Zhuge Liang's wife was the daughter of Huang Cheng yan, a famous Xiangyang scholar. Pang Degong, Zhuge Liang's teacher, lives in the south of Xian mountain in the south of Xiangyang

City, and Sima Hui, his teacher, lives in the east of Xiangyang City. Pang Tong, Zhuge Liang's good friend, lives in White Sandbank, Xiangyang, while Xu Shu, Cui Zhouping, Meng Gongwei and other good friends lived in Tanxi, the west of Xiangyang.

At the end of the Eastern Han Dynasty, there were frequent wars in Wanxian County of Nanyang (now the downtown area of Nanyang) All the scholars in the Central Plains took refuge in Jingzhou (Xiangyang) Zhuge Liang's brother "took refuge in Jingzhou with his uncle Xuan and cultivated in the wild", while Zhuge Xuan attached himself to Liu Biao, the governor of Jingzhou. Liu Biao was stationed in Xiangyang. As Liu Biao's strategic adviser, he could not live in Wancheng (now Nanyang) more than 200 Li away. It was reasonable to live in Longzhong, more than 20 Li west of Xiangyang City. Especially since the second year of Jian'an, Wan City had become a strategic stronghold for the Southward attack under the control of Cao Cao, while Liu Bei's "Three visits to the cottage" took place six years after the southward movement to Jingzhou. It was impossible for Liu Bei to go in and out of Wancheng under the close control of Cao's army to seek for talents. In addition, according to the records, before Zhuge Liang came out of the mountain, his extensive interpersonal relationships were all those who lived in Xiangyang or nearby. Since there were buildings in Nanyang of the Yuan Dynasty to commemorate Zhuge Liang, in order to support Zhuge Liang's claim that he once worked or lived in Wancheng, some people had been trying to find out the information about Zhuge Liang's relatives and friends who lived in Wancheng (Nanyang) from the historical records, but until now, they had not found it.

Nanyang Wolong Hillock was very close to Nanyang City's urban district. You could ride a bicycle from Wolong Hillock for 20 minutes to the ruins of Wancheng city wall. It was impossible to live in seclusion at such a close distance. Longzhong was more than ten kilometers away from Xiangyang.

Gao Min, director of the Institute of history, Zhengzhou University, a discussion with Nanyang advocates on Zhuge Liang's farming: "Because he (Xi Zaochi) was Xiangyang and familiar with the history of Han and Jin Dynasties, he had a clear idea of Longzhong's geographical location and administrative area, and he had no tendency to compete for historical celebrities because Longzhong belongs to Xiangyang."

zhu 诸 29-553

Zhuge Liang

诸葛亮 (181~234) 中国三国时期蜀国大臣、政治家。字孔明。琅邪阳都（今山东沂南南）人。家世为二千石官吏。在汉末动乱，所以文武战乱注依荆州刘表，隐居南阳隆中（今湖北襄阳西），躬耕陇亩，自比管仲、乐毅。建安十二年（207）刘备顾访名，三顾草庐。亮拟定东联孙吴、西拒荆、益、南和夷、越，北抗曹氏，待机进图中原的隆中对策。为以后的蜀汉制定了总的战略，成为刘备主要辅佐。次年曹操南伐，他和江东周瑜、鲁肃共同努力，并率至东吴劝说。

Yi Zhongtian, a professor of Xiamen University, was invited to give a speech entitled "Three Kingdoms of Chu Han and Hubei" at Peking University. He said: "at that time, there was a post road (equivalent to the current expressway) between Nanyang and Xiangyang. The transportation and information were very convenient. At that time, Zhuge Liang lived in seclusion in Longzhong, not far from Xiangyang City. Now, Longzhong was also the seclusion of Zhuge Liang, which Henan and Hubei competed for.

Is Zhuge Liang from Nanyang or Xiangyang? In fact, Zhuge Liang lived in a place that was under the jurisdiction of Nanyang Shire at that time. Therefore, it could be called Zhuge Liang grass room in Nanyang at that time. However, the geographical location was very close to Xiangyang, only 20 Li away. So people in Xiangyang say it's Xiangyang Longzhong."

At the end of 1989, the Institute of history of the Chinese Academy of Social Sciences and the Department of history of Beijing Normal University jointly invited a total of 27 historical experts from various historical research institutions and institutions of higher learning in Beijing, and held The academic argumentation meeting about Zhu Ge Liang's reclusive place.

At the meeting, everyone agreed:

First, the historical records record that Zhuge Liang's seclusion land and farming land was consistent in Xiangyang Longzhong;

Second, in the late Eastern Han Dynasty, there were frequent wars in the area of Nanyang Wan (now Nanyang City), and scholars from the Central Plains took refuge in Jingzhou (Xiangyang) When Liu Bei thrice visited Longzhong, Nanyang's Wan belonged to the jurisdiction of Cao Cao; Jingzhou was Liu Biao's administration. Zhuge Liang's uncle and Liu Biao were old friends. Therefore, he and his uncle could only live in Jingzhou (Xiangyang), never in Wan (now Nanyang City);

Third, Zhuge Liang had made many famous teachers and friends in Xiangyang. All his relatives lived in Xiangyang. None of Zhuge Liang's relatives and friends lived in Wan of Nanyang;

Fourth, before the Yuan Dynasty, there were no documents and cultural relics about Zhuge Liang's seclusion in Nanyang city. After Yuan Dynasty, the memorial building of Wuhou Temple appeared in Wolong Hillock of Nanyang;

Fifth, The hermit place of Zhuge Liang, in ancient and modern history, was not a problem without any doubt.

In view of the above reasons, it would be unanimously recognized that Zhuge Liang was engaged in Xiangyang Longzhong, but not Wolong Hillock in Nanyang.

Liu Bei and Zhuge Liang's "Longzhong countermeasure" article in biography of Three Kingdoms Zhuge Liang and Zhuge Liang's "Memorial before departure" in the newly compiled junior middle school Chinese textbook of people's education press interpret the "Nanyang" of "I used to be a common man, farming in Nanyang Shire" as "in the present Xiangyang area". The editor of the society listed historical materials such as Chen Shou's Records of the Three Kingdoms, Sima Guang's General Knowledge of Zizhi, Fan Wenlan's General History of China, Encyclopedia of China-Chinese history volume, and Ci Yuan (1979 version), all of which adopted the view that Zhuge Liang lived in Xiangyang Longzhong in seclusion.

In the notice of the State Council on Approving and transmitting the report of the

Ministry of construction and the Ministry of culture on the second batch of famous historical and cultural cities, issued by Guo Fa (1986) No. 104 on December 8, 1986, the State Council of China clearly pointed out that Xiangyang Longzhong was the former residence of Zhuge Liang and Nanyang was the memorial building, which made a scientific expression of the connotation of the two places of interest.

In the 1989 edition of the Collection of Words (Cihai), the explanation of long Zhongshan: in the west of Xiangyang County, Hubei Province, near the Hanjiang River. It was Zhuge Liang's former residence in the late Eastern Han Dynasty. About Longzhong's explanation: Zhuge Liang lived in seclusion in the late Eastern Han Dynasty (now Xiangyang west, Hubei Province), and Liu Bei visited here thrice in the 12th year of Jian'an.

The entry of Zhuge Liang in the Chinese Encyclopaedia clearly shows that In warlords fighting of the end of the Eastern Han Dynasty, Zhuge Liang with his uncle Zhuge Xuan went Jingzhou depend on Liu Biao, long in seclusion Nanyang Longzhong (now Hubei Xiangyang west)

To sum up, Nanyang Shire's jurisdiction over Longzhong at that time is an objective fact recorded in history, which has been confirmed and recognized by various historical materials in 1,800 years. Zhuge Liang's reclusive land and farming land are located in Longzhong, Xiangyang. "Zhuge Liang went to Longzhong of Xiangyang first, and then to Wolong Hillock of Nanyang", or "Zhuge Liang's seclusion was in Longzhong of Xiangyang, and his farming land was in Wolong Hillock of Nanyang" were not supported by historical data. Whether Zhuge Liang had traveled Nanyang city or not could not be found in historical records, but Zhuge Liang had never lived in seclusion or worked in Wolong Hillock in Nanyang city.

Chapter 8-Zhuge Liang's works

Longzhong Countermeasure

Since the dictatorship of Dong Zhuo, numerous powers had arisen in various regions and areas across the country. Compared with Dong Zhuo, Cao Cao was far lower-statured and had far fewer militaries. The reason why Cao Cao could defeat Dong Zhou lies not only in the favorable time, but also in his competent think tank. Now Cao Cao had an aggregate of some one million soldiers and was holding the king as a captive to control all powers in the country. Therefore, it was unwise to fight with him directly for the time being. Sun Quan's family had dominated Jiangdong Region for three generations. Jiangdong was a place with sophisticated terrains and people there were living well-off. Moreover, Sun Quan was a wise lord who knows to employ eligible people. Therefore, we could only turn to him for help instead of invading his territories. Jingzhou County was adjacent to Han and Mian River in the north, coastal areas in the south, Wu County and Kuaiji County in the east, and Ba and Shu County in the west. So as you could see, Jingzhou was actually a militarily strategic territory, but its owner, Liu Biao was not able to keep it. Therefore, it was literally a grand opportunity for you! Don't you want to overtake this county? Yizhou was a steep-landscaped place with vast and fertile lands in Ba and Shu County. The first king of Han Dynasty relied on this place to establish his imperial cause. Yizhou was really a highly populated region with abundant natural resources, yet its owner Liu Zhang had not cherished it. Most elites there were looking forward to serving an enlightened lord. My lord, you were the descendant of the royal family and enjoy a renowned reputation around the country for hospitably welcoming great heroes and gifted masterminds. So if you could occupy Jingzhou and Yizhou County, safeguard the vital passes, forge a sound relationship with the minorities in the west, appease the minorities in the south, form an external union with Sun Quan and conduct internal political reform, once the situation changes, you could dispatch a senior general to lead the armies in Jingzhou to the Central Plain while you yourself could lead the Yizhou armies out of Qinchuan! I believe all the people in Qinchuan would happily embrace you with food and wine! If you could follow my advice above, you were doomed to succeed and the royal family of Han Dynasty could be revived.

An Edict to Attack Wei for the Later Emperor

Note: This was an imperial edict written in the name of later emperor Liu Chan by Zhuge Liang.

Since ancient times, the way of heaven and earth had been blessed by benevolence, and brought disaster by lewdness. It was common sense that those who accumulate good prosper and those who accumulate evil decline. Therefore, Shang Tang and Zhou Wu King became king because of virtue cultivation, and Xia Jie and Shang Zhou King died out because of cruelty. The Han Dynasty now begun to show signs of decay, net of the law was too loose, resulting in treacherous evil people were not punished. Dong Zhuo caused disaster and the capital was in turmoil. Then Cao Cao created disasters, stole the country's power, oppressed the people outside, and usurped the hearts of the people inside. Cao Pi was determined to set up another flag, dare to create disaster, changed policy, stole the country's power, and people and gods were angry and denounced their murders. At this moment, the world of the Han family was like a star hidden, dark, ownerless, in danger. In this way, the world of the Han family wi ll undoubtedly fall. Liu Bei, our Lord, was wise and virtuous. His political and military achievements had come to the fore. He had helped the country to calm the chaos, start from many aspects and all people's wills unite like a fortress. The common people support it, respond to the times, build up the country and become the emperor, inherit the greatness, all neglected matters were handled, restore the world of the Han family, safeguard the Han family's principles and disciplines, and revitalize the Han Dynasty. Now, the world was not quiet, but the superstar was down. Liu Chan was young, but I inherited the great unification and unswervingly carried forward the great cause. Although I not yet familiar with the teachings of Guming minister, I cherished the essence of the country. The world was chaotic, the state was not clear, there was no peace. I was determined to carry on his predecessors, unfortunately the situation had not changed, so I was worried. I stayed up all day and did not dare to slack off. I reduced the expenditure of the harem to help the public, advised the rich to help the poor, farming and storing enough food to make people rich, appoint talented people and was able to accept elegant words, disciplined himself, our Shu Kingdom marched in and attacked the enemies of Cao Wei, our military's flag had not been raised, Cao Pi had died of illness, which means that he can't live if he did evil. The remaining evils of Cao Pi's fellow party were now doing bad things again, the bad root had not been thorough removed. The Prime Minister Zhuge loyal and devoted, worry about his country. The first emperor entrusted the whole world, and assisted Liu Chan. I ascended the altar to worship and granted prime minister Zhuge the commander of the three armies and responsibility for handling affairs on the spot. He led 200,000 cavalry, It was in this way that he take over the military power, attack the enemy with the would of heaven, eradicate the scourge and restore the former capital, success or failure was in this battle. In the past, Xiang Yu, the General Commander of the army, attacked the city and occupied the land. His ambition was not small, but he was defeated in Gaixia. He died in East City. His clan burned down and was laughed for thousands of years. All these were caused by against the would of the people. Today, bandits Cao Cao follow the example of Xiang Yu. It was the right time for us to crusade against the enemy according to the would of heaven. I hope God and ancestors bless us. We could win as long as we fight. Sun Quan, the Wu King, always was compassionate to the whole world, They would surround and ambush the enemy's army together with us. All countries in Liangzhou had sent troops, Yuezhi, Kangju, huhou, Zhifu and Kangzhi were all dispatched. When our army would attack from the north. As long as we reward the three armies, the justice army would be able to defeat the enemy just division According to the leader of the army, the destiny was in the body, the people and the right division would be able to defeat the enemy. We were a just army. We had proper reasons to send troops. Justice was on our side. We would gain victory with unstained s words. The enemy's army would surrender to us. Therefore, in the battle of mingtiao, Chengtang's army won the victory of defeating Xia Jie without fierce battle. King Wu of Zhou decided to fight with King Zhou in Muye, making King Zhou's army surrender before the battle. Our military flag leads the way. We didn't need to be militarized when we cross the states and shires. If there were those who seek refuge to us, give food to our army, according to the code of law, according to the size of contributions, there were rules and regulations. If there were clans or ministers or officials of Cao Wei who could judge the situation and surrender, they would not be guilty. In the past, Fuguo broke off with his family and kept his family; Weizi left the Shang Dynasty, Xiang Bo surrendered to the Han Dynasty, he was granted a marquis for his foresight. This was a truth that had been proven in previous lives. If someone continues to be perplexed, help tyrants and disobey our orders, they would be killed on the day of breaking the city. We could declare that our emperor was merciful, forgiving others and mourning the dead. Prime minister Zhuge would also announce other laws and regulations to the world so as to comply with the wishes of our emperor.

Report Before Departure

My dear Majesty,

The late emperor had not accomplished half of his cause before he went to heaven. Currently the whole empire was divided into three parts and our country was fragile and at the edge of danger. Yet, our ministers were never sluggish in national affairs and our loyal soldiers were devoting their lives at the battlefield, for they had kept all the favors the late emperor had bestowed upon them in mind and wish to repay him by serving you devotedly. Therefore, it was wise of you to open your ears to those capable talents so as to extend the sacred virtues of your father and stimulate our soldiers' morale, rather than look down upon yourself and make improper remarks to hamper rectitude and practical remonstrance.

All the courtiers and soldiers in and out of the palace of the emperor should abide by the law without any exceptions. There should be no bias in exercising the practice of rewarding and penalizing. All wrongdoers and law-breakers, as well as those good-deeds doers should be receive punishments and rewards from the officers respectively, so as to demonstrate your Majesty's impartial and open administration. Always remember not to be partial to someone and ruin the consistence of the laws in and out of the court.

The Senior Officers like Guo Youzhi, Fei Yi, Dong Yu, etc, were all loyal and honest men who were promoted by the late emperor to serve you. My advice was that you, my dear Majesty, should consult them in all affairs in the court, whether it be big or small, before taking actions. By doing so you would surely had all the misdeeds and drawbacks corrected beneficially.

Xiang Chong was a good-virtued and easy-going general who was versed in military tactics. After he was tested in the past, the late emperor had spoken highly of his capabilities and he was elected by all others the Grand Commander. My advice was that you should consult him in all military matters. By doing so you would surely keep all armies in great harmony, render them exert their best talents.

Staying close with loyal ministers and keeping away from the mean ones was the reason why the Former Hans was so prosperous. Staying close with mean ministers and keeping away from mean ones was the reason why Latter Hans was overthrown. When the late emperor was alive and discussed this with us, he would sigh miserably at the stories of Emperor Huan and Ling. Si Zhong, Shang Shu, Zhang Shi, Can Jun(all were the official titles in that era) were all loyal and dedicated people. So I wish you, my dear Majesty, could stay close with them and trust them. Then the prosperity of our country would be soon approached.

I was originally an ordinary man farming in Nanyang, only to secure my humble life in this troubled time without any wish to join the nobles. It was the late emperor who overlooked my commonness and humbled himself to visit me in my shabby hut, consulting me about the current affairs modestly. I felt so grateful that

I promised to serve him since then. So I was appointed in the most critical moment when our armies underwent consecutive defeats and crises. It had been 21 years since then.

The late emperor acknowledged my prudence and confided the great task to me when approaching his end. Since then, I could not help worrying and sighing day and night, in fear that I could not accomplish the task given by the late emperor and ruin his wisdom. So I embarked on the expedition to the barren lands over River Lu. Now the Southern part of the nation had been quelled and we had plenty of military resources. So it was high time that we should lead our armies to the Northern part. I would exhaust my poor talents and capabilities to wipe out all wicked people and restore the Han Dynasty and our old capital. That what I was obliged to did to manifest my deepest gratitude to the late emperor and you, my dear Majesty. As with the decision making and advice proposing, it was Guo Youzhi, Fei Yi and Dong Yun's duty.

I strongly desire you, my Majesty to assign to me the task of suppressing the rebels and restore the Han Dynasty. If I fail, I was willing to receive punishment to soothe the soul of the late emperor. If you hear no practical advice, then it was those advisers who were to blame. You, my dear Majesty should also spare no effort to come up with the right ideas, ask for advice by yourself, adopt the right suggestion and keep what your father said in mind. Then I would feel more than grateful to what you had done!

Now I was about to depart on a long march. I blinded by my own tears before this letter and had no idea what I had said.

Second Report Before Departure

The late emperor in consideration of Shu Han and Cao thief could not coexist and that its imperial activity ought not be contented with the enjoying of one-sided peace and tranquility, the late emperor instructed your minister me to had the insurgents suppressed. His Majesty, though fully aware of your minister I's inability to carry out this instruction, trusted me without hesitation; for the trend of events was that should the rebels not be quelled our imperial destiny would be bound to go to rack, so it would seem far much better to fight against them than succumb to them without resistance.

Upon receiving His Majesty's order, your minister I was quite lost in thinking, enjoying no sound sleep and having no good appetite. Your minister I was of the opinion that in order to be able to dispatch an expeditionary force to the north, it was essential that matters should first be settled in the south, and your minister I therefore ventured to cross the Lu River in the lunar May, entering right into the barren region and setting a dietary limit to himself. It was not your minister I did not know how to care about himself, but that the imperial dignity should not tolerate the maintenance of one-sided peace in Szechuen; this was where your minister I had endeavored to act upon the late emperor's instructions, though at my own risk. Such a course of action there are, however, many who were now disposed to criticize or deprecate.

Now the rebels were being engaged in the east and getting exhausted in the west; this was certainly a most propitious time to start a campaign, for taking advantage of the adversary's misfortunes was a good policy in military tactics. Your minister I begs to submit my views as follows:

With the acumen of Kao Ti — which could be likened to the brilliancy of the sun and moon — and with the counsels of his wise advisers, peace and order was not maintained until many difficulties had been surmounted and untold sufferings sustained. Seeing that Your majesty was not such as Kao Ti and Your Majesty's advisers were not such as Chang Liang and Chen Ping, how was it possible to expect to win, while sitting tight and making no attempt to move? This the first point not understood by your minister I.

While holding their respective counties, Liu Yu and Wang Lang always quoted from the sages in discussing the situation and in laying their plans, but they were so prone to suspicion and so easily overwhelmed with fear that they failed to make up their mind to fight year after year, until Sun Tse began to rise and annex the entire territory of Kiangtung. This was the second point not understood by your minister I.

Notwithstanding the fact that his resourcefulness was almost superhuman and his proficiency in strategies could favorably be compared with that of Sun Ping and Wu Chi, Cao Cao was once besieged at Nanyang, then escaped narrowly from Wuchao, then suffered seriously at Chilien, and was finally vehemently pursued at Liyang. At PeisLan he was nearly put to rout; at Tungkwan his escape from death was by a hair-breadth. After all this, he was only able to find himself settling down to enjoy temporary peace. Now in the case of one of much weaker caliber such as I, how could settlement be expected without having to go through dangers? This was the third point not understood by your minister I.

In his attacks on Changpa on five different occasions Cao Cao was repulsed; in his attempt to cross Lake Chao for four times he met with no success. He employed Li Fu and Li Fu betrayed him; he trusted Hsia How and Hisa How was killed. He was admired by the late emperor for his ability, yet he could not avoid such failures. Then how could one of I's inability be sure of success? This was the fourth point not understood by your minister I.

It was only a year since I came to Hanchung. During this time, however, generals such as Chao Yun, Yang Chun, Ma Yu, Yen Chih, Ting Li, Pai Show, Liu Ho, Teng Tung, etc., and seventy odd majors and garrison commanders had been dead, together with over a thousand brave generals of foreign birth and well-disciplined cavaliers. They were among the best of the elements, not belonging to one district only, but gathered together from various sources in all directions during the last tens of years. If it happens that another few years were allowed to pass without any action being taken, the result would be that two thirds of these elements would had been lost. Then with what would the enemy be attacked? This was the fifth point not understood by your minister I.

The people were now impoverished and the military strength was on the wane, yet we cannot afford to rest satisfied with the present condition of affairs. Under the circumstance, it would seem to involve the same amount of energy whether we stand still in the rear or take the offensive at the front. It is, therefore, inexplicable that while few appear to be prepared to take time by the forelock, there were many who were content with the keeping of one district to stand face to face with the rebels. This was the sixth point not understood by your minister I.

It might be stated that it was exceedingly difficult to bring the current of events to a standstill. At the time when the late emperor was signally defeated in Hupeh, Cao Cao chuckled with glee at the impression that the situation began to be settled in his favor. But later, when His Majesty threw in his lot with Wu and Yueh in the east acquired Szechuen in the west, and launched a campaign in the north resulting in the killing of Hsia How, it appeared likely that Cao Cao's plan was doomed to failure, while that of Han was going to be crowned with success. Shortly afterwards, however, Wu broke off its agreement; Kuan Yu lost the day; the late emperor got the worst of it at Tzukuei and Ts'ao Pei assumed the title of emperor. All this goes to show how this course of things was often too uncertain to admit of forecast. Your servant, therefore, desires to did all he can, even to the last drop of his blood, but without being able to foretell the consequences.

Report on impeachment of Li Ping

Since the death of the first emperor, Li Ping and Li Yan had taken care of the housework with their hearts, and did some small favors for others to do. They had been seeking fame without worrying about the state affairs, which was inconsistent with their official duties. Now I'm going to fight in the north, and I'm going to take Li Ping's soldiers and horses to guard Hanzhong. Li Ping was trying to find a way out. He's not obedient. Instead, he absurdly asks for five counties to be assigned to

Bazhou. He was the governor of Bazhou. Last year, I planned to march to the West and dispatch Li Ping to be in charge of Hanzhong. Li Ping said that Sima Yi had prepared a mansion for him and planned to summon him and give him official position. I know Li Ping's despicable private affairs. He wanted to take advantage of my departure, he told me the conditions to force me to comply and let him profit from it. In order to take the overall situation into consideration, I applied for Li Feng, Li Ping's son, to be in charge of Jiangzhou. Your Majesty, you had approved and granted him grace and trust. Such treatment focuses on the overall situation of the northern expedition. Up to now, Li Ping had been passing the buck. All the officials blame me for being too indulgent. It was precisely because the great cause of the northern expedition was uncertain and the Han Dynasty was in decline. At that time I thought, compared with grasping seize Li Ping's shortcomings, It's better to praise his merits. However, Li Ping was still obsessed with vanity and fame. It's unexpected that Li Ping can't be divided into public and private. If the facts of the audit were retained and not dealt with, the program of the royal court would be corrupted. The responsibility lies in me. It's my oversight. In the past, I praised him more and punished him less.

My deathbed Report

Lying on the ground, I feel that my natural disposition was clumsy and upright. In the face of the difficulties of the times, I led my division in the Northern Expedition and failed to succeed! Why was I so sick and dying at this time? I sincerely hope that your majesty could keep his heart and soul clear, restrain yourself from caring for the people, respect the first emperor to filial piety, give benevolence to the world, promote the hidden and disappeared talents, let the virtuous people come to the court, abandon and oust the crafty and slanderer, and let the social customs be honest and kind. When I was serving the first emperor, I relied on the government for money and had no money to create my own life. Now my house was in Chengdu. There were 800 mulberry trees and 50 hectares of land. They could did their own work and create extra grain to support themselves. I live in nonlocal, and I had no other dispatching expenses. I rely on the government for my daily food and clothing, and I had no other superfluous source to deal with my life, so as to increase my wealth. If at the time of my death I did not allow myself to had any extra money in my family or outside, I would had failed to live up to your Majesty's grace.

Self-deprecation Request for Jieting

Your minister I with a very weak talent, dominated in positions I shouldn't occupy. I lead the army to control the supervision and the power of life and death. I always train the three armies strictly. However, due to the failure to publicize military orders, teach laws and regulations, and be careful in case of emergency, Ma Su violated the orders in Jieting, failed in the battle, and failed in the vigilance of Jigu ambush. All the mistakes were caused by my improper appointment. In the book of spring and Autumn Annals, it was recorded that the commander in chief was responsible for the defeat of the army, and my position was just responsible for this crime. I asked myself to be demoted to the third grade to supervise my crime.

On the funeral of empress Gan

Emperor, you miss the mother of a nobility for her integrity and benevolence. She was virtuous and follows her inner chastity. When first emperor was general Zuo, the first emperor and his concubines worked together to cultivate and nurture your majesty you. The life of his wife was not long. When the first emperor was alive, he was deeply affectionate to his wife, loyal and cherished. He thought that the coffin of his wife would flutter in a distant place when the emperor missed her, and he specially sent envoys to welcome her back. When the first emperor died, the coffins of the first emperor and the first lady that the emperor missed had arrived, and the coffins of the first emperor and the first lady were all on the way. The mausoleum would be built, and the date of burial had been determined. I discussed with other ministers such as Lai Gong, Taichang Qing. According to the book of rites, it was the filial piety that should be observed by the people to cultivate benevolence from their relatives. To establish respect begins with respect for one's elders, which was to educate the people to abide by the rules. Don't forget your relatives, they had been born. In the spring and Autumn Annals, mothers value their children. Liu Bang, the former Emperor of the Han Dynasty, followed up and reburied his mother as empress Zhaoling; Xiaohe Emperor Liu Xun ceremoniously reburied his mother, Liang Guiren, in 91 AD, and honored his mother as empress Gonghuai; Emperor Xian of the Han Dynasty also reburied his mother, Mrs. Wang, and honored his mother as empress Linghuai. Now, when your majesty misses the mother of a nobility, she should had an honorary title to comfort the cold suffering of yearning in the underworld. I immediately waited for the respectful documents with the ministers. According to the posthumous law, she should be called empress zhaolie. According to the book of songs, the grain and husk of rice live in two places respectively, and the two people who love each other would be buried together when they die. Therefore, empress zhaolie should be buried together with Liu Bei, the first emperor. I would like to invite you to offer a ceremonious sacrifice to the ancestral temple and announce to the world. According to the etiquette, I would additionally report.

Reply to Du Wei

Cao Pi usurped the throne, killed some people loyal to the Han Dynasty and made himself Emperor. It's like a dragon made of clay and a dog made of straw. Because of his wickedness and hypocrisy, I want to destroy them in the name of justice with all wise men. Complain that you did not come to teach me earlier, and then want to go return to the mountain village and live in seclusion like you. However, Cao Pi built a large number of civil engineering projects again, recruited a large number of migrant workers to serve in the labor force, and grumblings of the people were heard everywhere. The first purpose of using these projects was to seek comfort and pleasure, and the second was to target Wu, Chu and other places. My heart was worried about the world, I can't see it. Now because of Cao Pi's many things, and because of this reason, we temporarily closed the border, let the people work hard in agriculture, cultivate crops and livestock, so as to benefit the people's livelihood, and punish and train soldiers, so as to wait for Cao Pi's mistakes or setbacks, and then attack him. In this way, the soldiers did not need to go through too much sacrifice, and the people did not need too much labor, so that the world could be pacified. You only need to use your virtue to conform to the arrangement of the deity to auxiliary behind the emperor. You were not required to take on military duties. Why did you want to leave so eagerly?

Reply to Li Yan

You and I had known each other for a long time, but you and I didn't really know each other You had just taught me to take the great country as my duty, and at the same time, be vigilant and not stick to some rules and regulations. This reason was true, but add to me nine kinds of the highest reward, it was absolutely impossible. We had a conflict because I didn't acquiesce in it. I used to be an ordinary person in the countryside. The first emperor looked up to me. He accidentally put me in an important position, making my position above ten thousand people under one person, and the salary given to me exceeded ten billion yuan. Nowadays, the northern expedition had not shown any effect. The former Emperor was kind to me, but I didn't repay the former Emperor. It's just like the Zhou Dynasty favoured the state of Qi and the state of Jin, while the Duke of Qi and the Duke of Jin both wanted to dominate the country, regardless of the state, but let themselves be noble and bigger, which was not moral. If we could wipe out the state of Wei, behead Cao Rui, and let the emperor go back to the place where he used to live, and share the glory with the ministers and the people, then Even if the emperor and give me ten kinds of highest reward I could accept, let alone give me nine kinds of highest reward?

Letter to Zhang Yi

When you were in Liu Zhang's place before, the surrounding environment was not good, which made me feel very bad. Later, when you were abducted to Sun Quan's place, I was also very sad and I could not sleep peacefully at night. When you come back, The state appoints you to an important position. I hope you and everyone could work together to repay the royal family and build the country. I think my friendship with you, as the ancients said, was as strong as stone. The way of our friendship was to give you my sincere heart to benefit you; cut off a piece of meat from my bone, let you eat, let you live, to increase your strength and make your eyes brighter; but didn't say thank you to me. What's more, my inner thoughts only said to Liao Hua, not to you, I understand you, you had endured so many sufferings, how could you not understand my mind?

Letter to Sun Quan

The Han Dynasty was unlucky, The law and discipline in the royal court was corrupt and unconstrained. Cao Cao usurped the throne. Today, all the people with lofty ideals wanted to exterminate him, but they did not form a unified alliance. I was entrusted by Emperor zhaolie. How dare I not did my best. Now the army had gathered in Qishan, and the rampant rebels would be wiped out on the side of the Wei River. I hope you would deal with the matter with the great justice of the alliance. I would order the soldiers to march northward to form the formation of encirclement with you. We would work together to pacify the Central Plains and help the Han Dynasty. I hope you understand the truth and learn from the past and the present.

A Letter Admonishing My Son

This was a way of life for a man of virture: to cultivate his own character by keeping a peaceful mind, and nourish his own morality by a frugal living. Only freedom from vanity could show his own lofty goal of life; and only peace of mind could help his own to achieve something lasting. To be talented, one ought to learn; and to learn, one ought to had a peaceful mind. One cannot develop his talent without learning, and one cannot accomplish his learning without peace of mind. Frivolity would prevent one from going deep into learning, and impetuousness would prevent one from moulding a noble character. One's age would flee with time, and one's ambition would wane with each passing day. If he did not exert himself in time, his mind would wither away like flowers and he would become a good-for-nothing in the world. And in the end, he could only perch in his humble dwelling, lamenting for his lost prime that would never come back to him again.

A Letter Admonishing My Nephews

A person should set up a lofty ideal, pursue the sages, control the lust, get rid of the worldly thoughts that were stuck in your own heart, so that the noble ambition that was almost close to the sages could be clearly reflected in your own, so that your own heart would be shocked and understood. We should be able to adapt to the test of smooth, tortuous and other different situations, get rid of the entanglement of trivial affairs and feelings, consult others extensively, and root out our own feelings of resentment. After doing this, although it was possible to temporarily stop in business, how could it damage your noble interests and why worry about the failure of your business! If the ambition was not firm, the ideological realm was not open, indulge in secular personal feelings, mediocre, always mixed in the mediocre crowd, it would inevitably fall into the inferior society, become the person who had ill bred and no future.

Announce revoke the post of Laimin

General Lai min once said to his superiors in public, "what merit did the new comer have? And what about honor and reward? Why did people hate me? Why was that?" Laimin was old and confused. He was crazy and unreasonable. When they first occupied Chengdu, some people thought that Laimin was easy to cause trouble and was not conducive to unity. The first emperor was tolerant and magnanimous, to stabilize the people's minds as the best policy when he was a newcomer. So he accepted him and tolerated him. He did not use rules to restrain him. Later, when the later master was initially appointed prince, somebody recommended, we should appoint Lai min as the chief steward of the prince's family. However, the first emperor was not happy, but could not bear to refuse the recommendation. Now that the later Lord succeeds to the throne, I already know what kind of person Laimin was in private, encourages him to play his own advantages, and promotes him to the official position of offering sacrifices to the general. I'm a bit arbitrary about this, which violates the correct opinions of some people and the wishes of the first emperor to alienate someone. I originally thought I could encourage the good side and avoid the bad side, so as to follow the righteousness to guide Laimin. In fact, it didn't fulfill the wishes of all people. Now that he can't play a role, it's time to let him left and let him think about it behind closed doors.

Military Order Thirteenth

Before the expedition, people should go to the ancestral hall to pay homage to drums, banners, chariots, etc. on the day of the beginning of autumn to show respect for weapons and instruments, just as those who love horses respect horses; those who love swords respect swords, the army should also respect the equipment used in the war. The previous day, the chief mourner should write the sacrifice words. The chief mourner respectfully prays with the sacrifice words. If we come back after win victory, we should go to the ancestral hall to pray after we return. Fear the enemy and sacrifice the bells and drums with their blood. When praying in the ancestral hall in autumn, if there was any capture, we only need to read the prayer, and did not need to sacrifice the bells and drums with their blood. The words of prayer were as follows: I ✕✕✕, as a general, was ordered to call on such and such immortals as drums, banners, chariots, etc. my most respected thing was that your war equipment was used to correct immoral behavior and to eliminate harm for the people. If we had offended the Tianwei, please forgive us for using these devices. In a certain year, a certain month, a certain beginning of autumn, make this oath. Wash the livestock, kill the livestock, take some clean grain, food and other things, respectfully hold the wine cup full of wine, pray to deity of god, dedicate to deity of god, thank deity of god.

The Art of War

Know what oneself like, know what oneself did not like, know what justice is, know what injustice is, so that you could command troops to fight. Therefore, the general who were good at commanding troops should learn from the things he did not like and cultivate and love those things he likes. It's impossible for soldiers to be all elite, horses to be all excellent, weapons to be all solid, once in a while, we need to know. The soldiers could be divided into the first-class, medium and inferior, there were three flexible ways to use them in war. Sun Bin said: use your inferior horse to deal with his superior horse; use your medium horse to deal with his inferior horse; use your superior horse to deal with his medium horse. In this way, two wins in three games. But here we were talking about the marching and fighting, not to say horses. We know the truth of using inferior horse to deal with superior horse. This time, it was impossible to win. We choose to give up. The enemy used the middle horse to fight against our superior horse, and the lower horse to fight against my middle horse. If we didn't win at first, wouldn't we win two battles in a row? If we could win and need to give up something, then we was willing to choose to give up something. There were three ways to win. Three strategies were to choose to lose one game in order to win two games. Guanzi said: on the one hand, it's hard to defeat the enemy when attacking the enemy's advantages. After a long time, our army would be very tired, and the enemy would be very strong. On the other hand, the enemy's disadvantages would make our army feel stronger. On the other hand, when attacking the enemy's weakness, it's easy to defeat the enemy and defeat the strong enemy. On the one hand, the advantage of the enemy was not shown, so it means that On the one hand, the enemy had advantages, and in our army's view, they were all weak. On the other hand, the enemy's strong side had become relatively weak. If we did not attack from the weak side of the enemy, the whole world would be a strong enemy.

War Strategy First

When our army was close to the enemy, the outpost in charge of liaison should start at dawn, stop within five kilometres from the enemy, and arrange the secret outpost according to the path that had been investigated and contacted on the left and right sides, which was also within five kilometres. A few kilometres away, five people in a group, each holding a white flag, stood at a high place, facing the direction of the enemy, stood to observe and look out. From the outside, they ought to also be in a hidden place. When the troops arrived, the outpost continued to move forward while looking for high places to continue to observe. The first soldier who see the enemy, pass the message on to the second, the second to the third, and so on. The first soldier rushed back to report to the leader of the army and told him what he had observed. If you see an enemy force of less than 100 people, you only need to use the flag to give an early warning; if you see an enemy force of more than 100 people, you need to raise the flag and shout out the warning at the same time, and the leader of the army needs to send a quick horse sentry to observe the situation, so as to report back.

War Strategy Second

When a troop needs to set up a camp, it ought to first send a trusted sentry and local guide to investigate the surrounding situation. Each squad ought to first send a messenger to determine the location of the camp, roughly determine the area occupied by the number of troops in each department, and determine the favorable terrain for observation before moving the camp. Then a team of sentinels would be sent forward, holding five color flags. Yellow flags would be planted in places where there were gullies and ridges. White flags would be planted in places where there were all directions. Black flags would be planted in places where there were rivers and streams. Blue flags would be planted in places where there were swamps and woods. Red flags would be planted in wild mountains and mountains. They would respond to each other with the sound of their own gongs and drums. Set up drums and flags so that you could hear each other. If you need to sneak across rivers and mountains, and a small group of elite cavalry forces enter the search state, you should be quiet within a few kilometres, without leaving footprints around. On the top of the mountain and the top of the tree, the troops would arrange sentinels, investigate and watch, and send small squad to guard the critical road in four directions. Then divide the troops into front and back teams, echelon guard and groped forward, and then arrange the placement of baggage, food, equipment, etc. the infantry in front and cavalry in the back ought to be neat and quiet, so as to prevent the sudden attack of the enemy. Neither the soldiers nor the horses could make noise or lose the queue. In case of a dangerous situation, it was necessary to take a convenient path, and order the troops to pass in order, or detour around. Turn the back team into the front team and the left team into the right team. They pass in order and stand in order like wild geese. Arrive at the place where the front stops, send a small group of cavalry to the southeast, northwest and four directions to spread out and stand and look out, and then set up camp in order. One by one, how many people and horses were arranged in a camp, time calculation, etc. all need to be reported in a list. Set up a big flag, 9 meters tall, and use it as time calculation. Don't let the time calculation be wrong. Use Zhuque flag for 11 am, white tiger flag for 5 pm, Xuanwu flag for 11 pm, Qinglong flag for 5 am, and call flag for central position. Firewood cutting, horse feeding, cooking and eating should not exceed the prescribed time boundary line.

Comment Emperor Guangwu

Cao Zhi said: Liu Bang, Emperor Gaozu of the Han Dynasty, and Liu Xiu, Emperor

Guangwu of the Han Dynasty, both rose from cloth clothing. The disadvantage of Gaozu was that it ignores details. The advantage of Guangwu lies in its knowledge and understanding. Gaozu rarely had the demeanor of a gentleman, he peed in the hat of the Confucian scholars, this kind of behavior could not be said to respect the Confucian scholars. Empress LV dotes Shen Shiqi, and licentious the harem. It was well known that Liu Bang appointed Shen Shiqi as the marquis and allowed him to indulge in licentiousness. The reason why Yao and Shun governed the country was that they advocated poetry, books, rites and music, which was despised by Gaozu. The reason why King Wen of Zhou was loved by the people was that he followed the Yin Dynasty etiquette and attached great importance to poetry, books, rites and music, while emperor Gaozu despised intellectuals and did not use this method. Gaozu listening to Qi Ji's flattering words, Qi Ji was bewildered by Qi Ji's beauty and prolonged solitary patronize Qi Ji, which led to the Imperial Palace competing for favor and calculating with each other. Empress LV killed Qi Ji cruelly. Empress LV tied Qi Ji up like a pig and locked her in a pigsty. At last, Qi Ji's hands and feet were cut off cruelly. Such a thing was abhorrent, was not lack of wisdom and consideration, such a thing was not as good as ordinary people. Emperor Guangwu was very knowledgeable, benevolent and wise. He was in charge of fighting against violence. He raised the banner of justice and led the righteous soldiers to wipe out the ugly forces. In the battle of Kunyang, he defeated Wang Yi and Wang Xun. He led the troops, in the "Han Jin" this place beheaded prefect Zhou Fu and general Liang Qiuci. At that time, the world was in chaos. The vassals from all over the country watched, and the people from all over the country revolted constantly. There were several people who claimed to be the emperor, and more people wanted to be the emperor. Liu Xiu led the army to conquer the powerful enemy of Qi State in the East, making countless people of red eyebrow army surrender and become prisoners. Peng Chong hesitates to wait and see, with two hearts, and finally returns to obedience, such as falling stars. Pang Meng was killed for betrayal and Chu Xiao was killed for treachery. Gongsun Shu was exterminated because he was divorced from his heart and morality. The reason for such a victory was that Liu Xiu first formulated strategies in the court, then mobilized the people to join the army, and then started to march with strategies. At this time, the generals in the war and the ministers in charge of planning were rewarded and trusted by those who were ordered to act, and those who violate the orders were bound to be in danger of annihilating. Therefore, it was said that the strategies of emperor Hanguang's March were in his mind. Before he set out, he had a good plan and grasp of the victory. Therefore, Dou Rong's return to the Han Dynasty was due to the reputation and credit of Guangwu emperor. Ma Yuan immediately admired Guangwu emperor when he saw him.

But I Zhuge Liang said: Cao Zhi commented on Liu Xiu, Emperor Guangwu, saying that his generals were not as good as Han Xin and Zhou Bo, and his advisers were not as good as Zhang Liang and Chen Ping. When people talk about this theory, they think so also. I think, although Cao Zhi's remarks really want to praise the guangwudi Liu Xiu genius and virtue, but it belittles the generation of heroes. Why would I say that? We could look carefully at the 28 generals in Yuntai, and was no such person as Ma Yuan listed here, were loyal and courageous, with a variety of excellent quality and merit. If we comment fairly, they were not inferior to those great people in the early Han Dynasty. The reason why Zhang Liang and Chen Ping were particularly prominent was that Liu Bang's behavior was relatively crude, so Zhang Liang and Chen Ping were very trusted, and Han Xin, Zhou Bo could look very outstanding. As the saying goes: "Those who suggest changing the chimney and moving away the firewood had no merits and achievements, but those who were injured in the fire fighting became the guest of honor." It means persuading people to eliminate the factors that might lead to accidents and prevent accidents before they happen. Although this was a small remark, it could be used to describe them two persons. Emperor Guangwu, Liu Xiu, was brave and talented. No one could surpass him in strategizing. The rest just follow his command and work together. Guangwu praised Deng Yu and said, "Since I had Yan Hui, the students had been more close to me." He praised Wu Han said: "Anyhow there was general you could satisfy me. Your force and loyalty were beyond the reach of others. " When discussing with the ministers, he thought that Ma Yuan's idea always coincided with his own, which was the embodiment of Mingjun's deep understanding of his subordinates. Guangwu's generals were not inferior to Hanxin and Zhoubo, and its advisers were not inferior to Zhang Liang and Chen Ping. This was because Guangwu had a long-term vision, he wisely eliminated the factors that might had caused the accident in advance and take precautions. Liu Bang was careless, therefore, Chen Ping, Zhang Liang, Han Xin and Zhou Bo could make great contributions, that was to say, what they had was the credit of putting out the fire after it had happened.

Comment Abdicate and Wrest

Fan Li was regarded as a wise and farsighted move by later generations because he resigned from the position of senior official. Yu Xin was regarded as a great credit by later generations for giving up his high position and wealth. Taibo was called benevolence by later generations for avoiding the throne. Yan Xiao, who resigned as king and caused trouble to the country, was later considered to be muddle headed.

Yao and Shun were called saints because of their abdication. Emperor Xiaoai was regarded as stupid by later generations because he was mess with many underage girls. King Wu of Zhou Dynasty was called righteousness by later generations because he replaced Shang Dynasty. Wang Mang was called usurper because he substituted the Han family. Duke Huan of Qi dominated because of Guan Zhong. The state of Qin perished because of Zhao Gao. Although these events happened at different times or in different specific events, the truth was the same. People who know what to did could be inspired to find ways to make the country strong; those who were dim could only see chaos and humiliation.

Huangling Temple Records

I personally cultivated crops in Nanyang Shire, and happened to meet my lord Liu Bei, thrice visited my cottage, looking for me. The country was in a difficult situation, and The situation did not allow me to decline. He was kind to me and with me together planned national affairs. In this way, our relationship was getting closer and closer. He took me into the role of chief designer. Now, I was on my way to Shu, riding a yellow ox, enjoying the beautiful scenery. Rows of disordered stones stand tall, waves on the water beat against the bank one by one. There were huge stones standing in the river, tall and abrupt, arranged into three peaks. In normal times, flood control should follow the path formed by these three peaks. If it was not for heaven to help Dayu to control the flood, how could these three peaks be formed only by human power? I walk around watching and appreciating, and saw cliffs standing on the left side of the river, like mountains. There were pine trees and strange rocks on the cliff. The scenery was picturesque. Pay close attention, the cliffs on both sides of the river overlap and fluctuate, just like the appearance reappearance of immortals. The hair on the temples, beard, eyebrows, hats and clothes were as clear as painting. A big flag was set up in front of us, and a yellow calf was on the right, just like the team supervising the project started the mountain to guide the water. It's said in ancient times that Huanglong helped Dayu to control the flood, took nine years to succeed. I believe it's true, not nonsense. It's a pity that the former Huangling temple was ruined by waste. The immortal helped Dayu to open up mountains and roads for flood control. He didn't need to dig mountains and open roads with axes. People should set up temples here to sail along the fairway opened by the immortal. I'm interested in doing this again. I'll rebuild the temple name and call it the yellow cow temple. I use it to commemorate the gods of Merit, was counted as I pay homage to the gods.

Yin Fu Scriptures Preface

Zhuge Liang said: The fate we say depends on one's own ability. If one's ability was high, then one's destiny was strong. So the fate of sages was respectfully called the fate of heaven. The difference between man and Saint lies in the level of wisdom. So say: the sky was vast but had the spirit, the earth was broad but did not know to change. Reading Yin Fu Scriptures, we could know that nature was in our own hands, and life and death were determined by ourselves. The key to being human or holy lies in the perception and judgment of things. Those who had contributed to social development and contributed to the rise and fall of the world without leave their name. They were intelligent. Because of heaven's will, the Yellow Emperor was able to rise to heaven and become an immortal, the Shang Tang was able to be monarch, and the five hegemons in the spring and Autumn period could become princes separately. It's easy to find a minister and choose a monarch, but you can't make a decision easily. When Jiang Taigong was ninety years old, he didn't had no chance, because he was waiting for a wise monarch. If you could get the full help of a wise man, even if you set up a stone as your master and carve a piece of wood as your monarch, you could also get the world. The subjects were loyal to the monarch, but the monarch was suspicious of fear. If so, wasn't the monarch taking disaster on his own? Without a wise monarch, a person of high morality and principle would not be an official until he dies. It's better to get rid of your ambition and keep your duty, save your life and wait for the change of the current situation. People in the world think that Confucius was talented but not successful. Zhang Yisheng of Su and Qin met the time. Wrong! The aim of wise person was to settle down the country. How could they become a pawn who was ordered at will? This was the shame of those who know books and could write! In the future, talented and outstanding people should use their talents carefully. Fan Li lived a long life because of his prudence; Wen Zhong died because of his recklessness, was it not because he casually uses his ability to divulge the secret? People who divulge their secret would fall into three catastrophes (according to Buddhism, there were four catastrophes in the universe: success, living, destruction and extinction. People could only survive in living catastrophes.) We should did this. The sages hide their works in famous mountains and only pass them on to like-minded people. They hide them in cabinets so as not to be stolen by villains and used to did bad things.

Yin Fu Scriptures Explanatory Note

Person was person because of his natural nature. People's heart was the destiny that dominates the world. The "Tao" based on the world was the rule of man. Zhuge

Liang's note: I think based on heaven and earth, if the goal was determined to be a sage, the core lies in the inner joy, anger, sadness, laughter and desire, these five aspects.

No one in the world could see or know the man who stole the opportunity in advance. The gentleman (person of complete virtue) got it. Although the gentleman was poor, he sticks to his integrity. If the villain gets it, he would act recklessly regardless of his own life. Zhuge Liang's note: didn't Confucius and Jiang Taigong be more wise than Sun Tzu, Wu Qi, Han Xin and Bai Qi? Therefore, there was a difference between a gentleman and a villain. These four men were so brave that they were killed because they did not meet a wise monarch.

There was a magic "thing" between the heaven and the earth. It produces all things, time and space. The heaven's opportunity was hidden in the invisible. That magical "thing" was the wisdom of saints, that is, Tao. Tao was limitless, limitless generates Taiji, Taiji generates Liangyi, Liangyi was Yin and Yang. Yin and Yang correspond to each other, transform each other, supplement each other, and make everything in the world run normally. Liangyi produces four images. Spring, summer, autumn, winter; east, west, north, south; green dragon, white tiger, Zhu Que and Xuan Wu all were four images. The elephant was also the Tao. Heaven was always in favor of the Tao, so the sage would come to the world, and the sage would follow the Tao, deduce astronomical calendar, actuarial mathematical meteorology, and investigate good and bad. Then everything between heaven and earth, including ghosts and gods, yin and Yang, ordinary people, and the north and the south, was in the Tao, all inclusive. The Tao of the eight trigrams, telling and using it; 60 years a Jiazi, transmigration and circulation, the beginning of all things, metabolism, the unity of all things, were in the Tao.

If the gods kill, there were signs for the dragon and snake's activities on the land; if people kill, there would be signs for the surrounding environment. Note to Zhuge Liang: Xiang Yu killed tens of thousands of soldiers in the Qin state. The strong wind was dim and unknown. It lasted day and night. It was like earth shaking.

Sixteen Strategies

The Strategy of Governing the Country First

The key to running a country was like running a family. It's necessary to establish a foundation for housekeeping. If the foundation was right, the end would be right. Basically, it was the rules that were advocated first. At the end, follow and follow. The rules that started to be advocated were harmony between heaven, earth and man. With it comes everything. Without sky, man cannot exist, without earth, creatures cannot grow, without man, all things cannot succeed. Therefore, the rules issued by the monarch ought to be in accordance with the law of the development of things, just like the north star. There were some stars around it as the core, which were vaulted. The assistance under the stage was like the assistance of a minister. Many stars were like officials, and many small stars were like the common people. Therefore, the North Star cannot be moved at will, the assistant ministers cannot lose their manners, and the officials cannot easily make mistakes, which was the reason for the movement of celestial bodies. So, to build the platform, used to observe the astronomical weather; in the outskirts worship the gods, positive and negative ought to comply with the laws of nature, this was to regard the operation regular pattern of heaven as the fundamental. To cultivate crops, mountains, forests, rivers, society as a whole, were to take the nature of the land as the basis. To educate people to observe rites, book of songs and music, to set up schools above the Ming hall, and to build temples for ancestor worship within the high walls, were to take the human nature as the basis. Therefore, daily laws and regulations were fundamental, was the main point of the rules. The round tenon can't enter the square hole, and the pencil sharpener can't be used to cut trees. That was to say, it can't be successful to did things in a way that didn't conform to the laws of things; it can't play its role if it uses a function that didn't conform to the characteristics of the tool itself. Therefore, if the sky loses its regularity, there would be devils in the sky; if the land loses its regularity, the crops on the ground would wither and die; if the human loses its regularity, there would be disaster. According to the Book of Songs, "it was not that the decrees of the deceased first monarch should be absolutely obeyed, but that they should be viewed dialectically. If they were in line with the fact, they should be obeyed. If they were not in line with the fact, they should not be obeyed." That's why.

Monarch and Ministers Second

The political activities between the monarch and the ministers were like the regular pattern between the heaven and the earth. If the regular pattern between the heaven and the earth were correct, the harmony between the monarchs and the ministers would exist. The monarch ruled with benevolence, and the officials discussed the state affairs with justice. A minister with two minds cannot serve the monarch, and a person who doubts monarchy cannot authorize him to be a minister. If the leaders above and the officials below like politeness, the common people were easy to obey; if the upper and lower monarchs and ministers were harmonious and smooth, the "Tao" between the monarch and ministers would be available. You use etiquette to call on your officials, and your officials use loyalty to serve you. The monarch plans politics, the minister plans to carry out specific things. Politics was to govern the country in the right name, and ministers who did things were to persuade people to build up their careers.

When the monarch was in power and the minister plans to carry out specific things, the "Tao" of fame was built up. Therefore, the monarch was back to the north, facing the south, the monarch was Yang, the monarch gives orders; the ministers were back to the south, facing the north, and towards the monarch. The ministers were Yin and the ministers worship the decrees. The monarch make rules and regulations, make laws and policies, and the ministers implement laws and policies. If the legal system was implemented, it would be meritorious; if it was meritorious, the people would be rewarded with the blessings. Therefore, the three principles and six disciplines were divided into upper, middle and lower parts. The upper part was the monarch and minister, the middle part was the father and son, and the lower part was the husband and wife. They act according to their own rules, and then the blessing comes naturally. Between monarchs and ministers, etiquette was the basic link of connection; between father and son, grace was the relationship of connection; between husband and wife, and was the key to connect family peace. The leaders at the top and the officials at the bottom should not be disrespectful. If the upper part was not straight, the lower part would bend; if the upper part was confused, the lower part would rebel. Therefore, the monarch only needs to did the political work that the monarch should do, while the minister needs to did the job that the minister should do. Therefore, if the wise monarch was self-cultivation and diligent, the loyal minister would did things profitably. Those who study want teachers who understand the reason, and those who were officials want a wise monarch. Therefore, it was necessary to set up all kinds of official positions, large and small, arrange the salaries and titles of officials at all levels clearly, establish the politics of observing astronomy and meteorology and various systems, and set up three ministers and six ministers as auxiliary ministers, so as to avoid abandoning the public due to private affairs and interfering in politics due to evil things. This was the basis to govern the country.

Listen to All Kinds of Voices Third

As a monarch, to govern a country, we need to listen to all kinds of bottomed voices, observe all kinds of bottomed situations, we should see the details and listen to the voices of the bottom of the society. Small things were not easy to see, and the voice of the bottom of the society was not easy to hear, so the wise monarch sees the small things very big, and hears the voice of the bottom of the society very clearly, so that the external things could be handled well inside the palace, and the real external situation could be used to make the interior of the palace clear and correct. Therefore, to govern the country, we ought to listen to the bottomed voices, observe the bottomed situations, adopt everyone's correct opinions, and extend this method and plan to the next level of government and ordinary people. Then everything could be our own eyes, and everyone was our own ears, to assist government. So the Book of Songs says, "The sage had no fixed heart, but takes the people's heart as his own." What people see in their hearts was expressed by their eyes, what they want to say in their hearts was expressed by their mouth, what they hear in their hearts was transmitted by their ears, and what people feel stable was confirmed by their health. Therefore, if one had a heart, if the country had a wise monarch, it was very good to deal with the external affairs with the internal system and laws of the court and the harmony of humanity. Therefore, if one had a heart, just as a country had a wise monarch, it was very good to deal with external affairs by using the internal system of the Palace, decrees and human harmony. To observe the shape of the sun and the moon was not enough to say that it was the brightest; to hear the sound of thunder was not enough to say that you hear all, so a wise monarch could become wise by seeing more; and by listening more and not being blinded. There was no way to distinguish the gong sound from the Shang sound without having heard of the five sound levels of Jiao, Zheng, Gong, Shang and Yu; there was no way to distinguish the sky color from the earth color without having seen the five colors of blue, yellow, red, white and black. It's said that wise monarchs did things differently like day and night. The day was to did public things, at night was to did private things. Occasionally, some people sigh and complain, some things were not heard, some advice were not heard. If the voice of the wronged cannot be heard, the wronged cannot be vindicated; If the advice of the loyal ministers could not be accepted, the faithful would not be trusted, the evil treachery might succeed. So the Book of History says, "what the god could see comes from what I see for the people; what the god could hear comes from what I hear for the people." That's why.

Accepted the Recommendations Fourth

To govern a country, we should be good at accepting the advice of ministers and the people and adopting the strategies of the people. Therefore, the monarch had some ministers who directly advise, and the parents had some children who directly advise. When the behavior of the monarch or the parents was improper, the ministers or the children advise to point out, their mistakes could be corrected, let they become correct and perfect. Ugly and wrong things cannot support it; beautiful and right things cannot oppose it. If we obey the ugly and wrong things and oppose the beautiful and right things, then our country would be in danger. If the monarch refuses the minister's advice, then the loyal ministers were afraid to offer their excellent strategies, and the evil ministers might carry out their strategy, which was harmful to the country. Therefore, in a country of high morality, we should speak with integrity and did with integrity; in a country without morality, we should be careful in our actions and speak with caution, otherwise there would be danger; the leaders above cannot hear the truth, and the ministers below did not reflect the real situation. Therefore, Confucius was good at listening to the opinions of ordinary people. He didn't think it's a shameful thing. Duke Zhou didn't think it's a shameful thing to deal with ordinary people. So they all had works handed down to later generations, and later generations think that they were saints. So, the house was leaking, the water was ticking to the ground, and the way to stop the leakage was on the roof. If the roof didn't stop leaking, the house was uninhabitable.

Investigation and Suspicion Fifth

Investigation and suspicion were a means of governing the country, just as it was called to observe the color difference between red and purple, and listen to the tone difference between Gong Yin and Shang Yin. So purple red was easy to disturb red, and decadent music often confuse elegant music. It was easy to cause confusion in places where the law cannot be governed, and people's confusion might lead to suspicion of the state's administrative order. There were always different kinds of things, sometimes different things had the same color. White stones like jade were regarded as treasures by stupid people; fish's eyes were like jewels, which stupid people think were jewels and then those people put them as their own. A fox like a dog was often adopted by stupid people. Like watermelon gourd, stupid people often eat it as watermelon. Therefore, Zhao Gao identified a deer as a horse, and Qin II had no doubt about it; Fan Li presented Xishi, a beautiful woman from Yue, to Wu, which the king of Wu did not think was a disaster. If a plan was suspected, it cannot be sure; if it was suspected, it cannot succeed. Therefore, sages could only understand some things, but can't tell them. They ought to believe in divination and had this method to determine good and bad. The Book of History said: "Three people divination, the result should be the same judgment of two people." But people with great doubts, "when planning, they would consult ordinary people." Therefore, Confucius said, a wise monarch should not worry about others not knowing himself, but about himself not knowing others. When there was no foreign enemy invasion, people often didn't know the internal crisis, only worry about the internal world and didn't know the external world; didn't worry about the common people didn't know the meaning and claims of the monarch, just worry that the monarch didn't understand the minds and claims of the common people; didn't worry about the people with low status didn't understand the claims of the people with high status, just worry about the noble people didn't know the ideas and claims of the people with low status. Therefore, a gentleman would die for his confidant, a beauty would dress up for those who like him, a good horse would gallop for those who control him, and the god would point out a way for those who pray and bless themselves. Therefore, the trouble for a wise monarch to adjudicate prison cases and execute criminal law was that he can't see clearly. Some of them were innocent and regarded as guilty; some of them were guilty and forgiven; some of them were powerful people who force others to say the same thing, others dare not say more; some of them were the hatred of the poor people who were violated by others; some of them were just people who were wronged, some of them were unjust people who can't did justice, some of them were trustworthy people who were suspected; some of them were loyal people being framed; it's all because of violating the would of the god, and what happens in the folk, it's a sign of disaster, riot, disaster and danger. Only a wise monarch, when administering prison cases and executing criminal law, asks for the written papers and speeches of the parties, did not cheat, did not hide, did not bend, did not cheat; observes the contacts of the parties, investigates the advance and retreat of the parties, listens to the voice of the parties, and looks at the places that the parties pay attention to. The appearance was afraid, the voice was pitiful, the coming was quick and the going back was late, looking around and sighing and lamenting. This was the countenance of being wronged and unable to be vindicated. Look down, and secretly look around the situation, When they see others appeared very timid, and want to retreat, want to go back, when breathing lost to hear what others said, whispered to himself, hesitant and psychological thinking, language lost demeanor, come late, go back was fast, dare not look back, this was the performance of guilty people want to exempt their crimes. Confucius said: "the way to examine a person's behavior was to look at what he had experienced, to see what this person what could rest assured, and to think about it comprehensively. What was this person conceal? Why was this person conceal these?"

How to Manage People Sixth

The way to manage people was to make social customs and social atmosphere noble, simple and harmonious, and publicize these rules so that people all over the world know and comply with them. So some book says: display the ethics and social noble rules for the common people to follow; let the common people know the behaviors that the society advocates and the ugly behaviors of the society, and let the common people know what behaviors should be prohibited. The light of the sun and the moon could be looked up by all people; the world was big, and all things obey certain laws, so that all things had vitality. Therefore, emperors such as Yao and Shun, distant tribes of foreign nationalities, all paid tribute and submitted to them, while emperors such as Jie Zhou, even in China, were betrayed. It's not that god wants these people to did this, it's the result of the monarch's education of the common people. So governing the world and civilizing the people was like cultivating seedlings, cutting off the unnecessary things first. Therefore, if a country was going to prosper, it ought to begin with praising its people. Because its people could abide by laws, live in harmony and work hard, the country would prosper. The decline of a country usually begin with the praise of its carnal pleasures. Because the monarch likes carnal pleasures, and he likes rare treasures, he alienates the people. As time goes by, if the monarch lingers here, the country would die. When a wise monarch governs a country, he ought to know what the people were worried about and where they are. The people were afraid of the grass-roots officials with low status, because they control the fate of ordinary people. Although these officials were the tiny subjects of the country, they were actually very important officials of the country. Therefore, there was nothing that grass-roots officials dare not do. No one knows their limits. Good things could be done, and bad things could be done also. If these grass-roots officials steal money from ordinary people, if people can't bear the hunger and cold, there would be rebellion, which would force people to revolt. The only way to did this was to persuade the grass-roots officials not to occupy the time and season of plundering the people to sow and cultivate; as far as possible reduce taxes, not to exploit the people innocently and collect money, not to plunder all the people's food and money. If we could did this, the country might be rich and the people might be stable. Is it not better? As large as the country and as small as the ordinary people, they did not worry about poverty, but about instability and injustice. So Tang Yao and Yu Shun governed the country, made use of the harmony between people, used the weather and geography to prepare for the disaster year. In the autumn, they stored the surplus grain for the insufficient supply. When there was surplus money in the world, no one picked it up on the road and took it back. The common people did not go everywhere to find shelter, because there was no disaster. So spring and autumn five tyrants, it was not worth flattering how good. So now all the princes like the interests. If value orientation only pays attention to their own interests, the common people were scrambling for the interests. Disasters and hazards appear together. The powerful bully the weak, the number of people who cultivate themselves decreases, the number of idle people increases, the people's fickleness was like cloud drift, and the people's mind was unstable. The book says: "what's rare was not the lack of valuable things, but the fact that people didn't steal them; what's rare was not the lack of rich materials with small value, and what's rare was that people didn't get confused." Each department of the officials at all levels should take their own responsibilities and manage the responsibilities for their own bounden duty, which was the secret of the sage's governance of the country.

In the era of Qijinggong, the disadvantage was that people like luxury goods and did not follow the etiquette system. During the Zhou and Qin Dynasties, Remove some of the surface things, and tend to the nature of things, to persuade people to take into account more interests. Making some useless utensils and collecting some meaningless goods, such as gold, silver, Jasper, jewels, jadeite and strange stones, were all produced from far away places, which were not available to ordinary people. Embroidered Brocade, exquisite textile, silks and brocades, red and yellow beautiful clothes of all colors, none of this applies to farmers. It takes a lot of effort to carve exquisite utensils and make ingenious objects. All these hinder the farmers from farming the land, taking in and out of the carriages with exquisite exterior decoration, wearing fur coats and exquisite underpants, which were not what the farmers need to decorate themselves. There were several doors of the house, all of which were painted with beasts and other ornaments; the walls inside the house were very tall, and the tombs built very luxurious, spending all of their money, but in order to pursue vanity, this was not what the farmers need to live in the house. The book says: "What ordinary people like was to cultivate themselves, to work hard, to save money and to support their parents," We should restrict these people with the upper limit of money, educate them with the etiquette of poetry and books. the year of harvest could not be wasted, nor be too harsh on ourselves in the year of disaster. At ordinary times, there were certain savings and reserves. It was the way to manage the country to support children with the grain reserves. Isn't it also in line with the way of heaven and earth?

Take Measures Seventh

The policy of governing the country was to advocate the implementation of correct measures and the correction of wrong measures. Running a country was like health care. The principle of health care lies in mental health. The principle of running a country lies in recommending talented people. Therefore, mental health could make the country healthy, recommend talented people, and make them officials at all levels, so as to make the country stable and rich. Therefore, the state had talented people, just as a house had a roof beam column, the roof beam column cannot be too small, and the talented people assisting the state cannot be too weak; if the roof beam column was too small, there would be harm; if the talented people were too weak, the state would be in danger of overturning. Therefore, only when we advocate the right measures and correct the wrong measures, could the country be stable. Therefore, it was only with straight wood that the pillar could be solid, only by using honest and wise talented person could the country prosper. The straight wood comes from the quiet forest, and the integrity and wise talented person come from the public. It was necessary for the monarch to see, find and ask about the hidden places. Some people were talented, but lost in other countries. Wise people and ordinary people were in the same position, enjoying the same salary. Some people had brilliant talents and farsightedness. They didn't see the notice of seeking talents. There were loyal, wise and filial people, but there was no recommendation in the countryside. Some people live in seclusion and were not willing to go out of office. Some people take chivalry, justice and courage as their principles. Some people were loyal to the monarch and slandered by bad people. Tang Yao recommended hermits; Shang Tang recruited talents from a large number of people, and Duke Zhou adopted the suggestions of ordinary people, because he met the right people, so that the world was tranquil. Therefore, the monarch should use the means of reward to encourage his subordinates to make contributions, and use the appropriate official position to entertain the wise talents. He should not waste the talents selected from the common people to become officials. He should open up a wide range of ways to recommend talents, and take the rejuvenation and governance of the country as the foundation. To hire elegant hermit gentlemen, it was necessary to offer more munificent treatment, so that the common people might be convinced, and bad people might hide. If the appointed officials were not trained and selected according to the standards of governing the country, and the talents who had the standards of governing the country were not appointed as officials; no one sympathizes with poverty and ugliness, but everyone competes for wealth and beauty, the flatterers were satisfied with their ambition, the loyal and honest people were exiled to the frontier, not to be reused, if we didn't provide extraordinary treatment, how could we get the help of honest and wise talents? If the country was in danger and it was not managed in time, the common people cannot live in stability. This was the fault caused by the loss of integrity and wise talents. Since ancient times, there had been no wise minister to assist, and the country was not dangerous; the wise minister to assist, and the country was unstable, never before.

Setting up a special position for a relative household by opening a back door would cause chaos, selecting talents for a certain position by opening a back door would lead to social dissatisfaction. So it's just like marrying a daughter-in- law to hire talented people. Whoever had a high dowry price would be able to marry his daughter-in- law. Or, the woman accepts the dowry because she admires the talent of the man. In the same way, a gentleman accepts official positions because he appreciates the preferential treatment of the monarch, or because the monarch attaches importance to himself, so as could to establish his reputation. Only with generous treatment to hire wise talents, the state could be tranquil.

Examination and dethronion Eighth

The policy method of investigating the promotion and recall of officials was to promote excellent officials and recall incompetent officials. The wise monarch dare to show his heart to heaven, investigate and understand what was good and what was evil, and spread it to the whole country, covering the lowly officials and ordinary people. The promotion and appointment of wise people, the dismissal and dismissal of corrupt and timid people, so that all people could understand what was the standard of excellence, and understand and abide by the national laws and regulations, let many wise people gather like rain. This was the reason to advise people to did well and not to did bad things, and publicize the code of conduct for good and evil. Therefore, when examining the policies of promotion and removal of officials, it was necessary to know the human suffering. There were five aspects of disaster. Some officials with very small positions, who seek personal gain for business, commit crimes with power, hold power in their left hand, trample on people's livelihood with their right hand, invade the public's family internally and exploit the people externally, which was the first disaster. Some of them had been punished more severely, some had been punished less severely, laws and regulations were not fair, and those who had not committed crimes had been wronged, so that they had been killed, some criminals had been leniently dealt with, the powerful people had been safeguarded, the poor and weak people had been suppressed, all the people had been punished with harsh criminal law, and the unjust lovers had been wrongly blamed. This was the second disaster. Some officials connive at criminals, persecute the people who tell the truth, refuse other people's complaints, conceal the situation, plunder and rob property, and kill good people in vain. Although this kind of improper practice would not last for a long time, it was also not allowed. This was the third disaster. Some officials had changed their local posts for many times, and they also serve as assistants in local governance. They were partial to the people they like, unfair to the people they dislike, and misbehave. Some of them were loose in supervision, and they act recklessly. They take advantage of the opportunity of tax collection to collect money privately. They take advantage of the opportunity of persuading people to engage in farming and mulberry to exploit the common people. When they collect civil materials, they spend a lot of money, eat, drink, attach to officials, and withheld by false pretenses to become private property. This was the fourth disaster. Some officials were greedy for credit. They take advantage of the opportunity of rewards and punishments to make profits. They set higher price standards by themselves, charge more for buying and selling, and then retain part of it for themselves. This was the fifth disaster. The officials who had these five kinds of behaviors ought to be removed, and the officials who did not had these five kinds of behaviors could be promoted. So the book says: three years to assess the achievements of the government, remove the fatuous officials and promote the virtuous ones.

Govern the Army Ninth

The way to govern the army was a strategy to control the border, maintain the regime, and save the country. Taking the powerful army as the foundation of the country, killing the rioting princes and fighting against the rebellious subjects were the grand plan to protect the country and keep the society stable. Therefore, we need to had both culture and martial force. Therefore, the claws and teeth of bloodstained insects were useful. If you like each other, you could play together and subsist together; If you're afraid other side, you could protect yourself and attack other side. When there were no claws and teeth, people set up weapons to defend themselves. Therefore, the State takes the army as the fence to assist the national security, and the monarch takes the minister as the assistant; if the assistant was strong, the state was stable, if the assistant was weak, the state was dangerous, which lies in the strength of the appointed generals. A general who was not able to make decisions for the people might not be appointed as a general; a general who was unable to assist the country might not be appointed as a general; a general who was unable to direct a war might not be appointed as a general. Therefore, the government of the country needs the minister of culture as the auxiliary minister, and the military needs the generals who advocate military ethics as the auxiliary, which was the strategy of the military. Govern the country ought to consider external defense, governance army ought to consider internal strict discipline. For the domestic were the Han people, the abroad were Yi people. Yi people, difficult to enlighten by education, easy to obey the mighty force; etiquette could be used, mighty force could also be used. Therefore, the Yellow Emperor fought against the Yan Emperor in Zhuolu, the Tang Yao fought against the foreign people at the cliff water edge of Nanyang, the Ming clan was attacked by Shun, and the Hu clan was attacked by Yu. From the three emperors and five emperors to the present sagacious emperor, they all advocated moral education so wisely, but sometimes also had to use force. Therefore, war was evil thing, which could only be used when it was necessary. The method of fighting was to determine the strategy first and then carry out it. Examine the time and place, know the ideas of the people, let the soldiers be familiar with the use of training weapons, the rules of rewards and punishments should be made public, investigate and know the enemy's strategy, see the dangers on the march road, respectively understand the safety and dangerous places, occupy the reason of the subject and the guest, know the route of advance and retreat, find the chance to fight, set up the preparation for defense, strengthen the imposing manner of conquest, and develop the warrior. The potential of the army, the strategy of plotting for success or failure, the future of life and death, and then the general could lead the army to go out and spread the atmosphere of defeating the enemy. These were the major strategies for the army to fight. A general was a man who was in charge of the fate of soldiers and a weapon of the country. He first determines the strategy of operations and then implements it. His command was like the water of a waterfall, its capture was like a hawk and Falcon attacking prey, the army was like an open bow when it was quiet, and when it was moving, it was like the launching of a mechanism. It was invincible, even the powerful enemy was destroyed. If a general not think about worries in an all-round way, soldiers didn't had momentum and the army didn't work together, if they just purely think about strategies, even if there were millions of troops, the enemy was not afraid. If there was no hatred, did not resent the other side; if it was not the enemy, did not fight. If the project was not examined by Luban's eyes, and he did not know the subtlety of the project; if the strategy of the war was not planned by Sun Wu, and he did not know the operation result of the strategy. The plan ought to keep secret, attack the enemy ought to quick, capture the prey like hawks and falcons, and fight like a river burst the bank, then the soldiers were not tired yet and the enemy had broken up, this was the imposing manner of using the troops. So the generals who were good at fighting were not angry, and the generals who were good at winning were not afraid of the enemy. Therefore, the wise generals first make strategies for victory in strategy, and then fight; The general who didn't understand was to attack first and hope subsequent win. The victorious generals follow the method and constantly revise the path, while the defeated generals go astray and lose the way forward. This was the strategy of harmony and adversity. The general admired the power, the soldiers practiced hard and fought hard without any rash. Once they started to move, they would fall from a high place like a big round stone, and they would smash the enemy. It was impossible to rescue and stop them. So the enemy was not in front or behind, just under the stone. This was the momentum of using soldiers to fight. Therefore, the strategy of unifying troops in war was fantastic. It was based on unexpected wisdom. He could be soft and could also be strong, able to be weak and could also be powerful, could survive and could also escape, when it's fast stretches out like a river and sea, and when it's still, it's like Mount Tai, it's hard for the enemy to predict. It's unpredictable like Yin and Yang. It's boundless and abundant like the earth It was as full as the sky, and as inexhaustible as the water of the Yangtze River and the Yellow River, as the sun, the moon and the stars remain unchanged; it circulates at four o'clock in the morning, the day, the night and the night, and it was hard to predict life and death; the prosperity and decline of the gold, wood, water and fire land alternate in turn, and the odd and the right were mutually reinforcing, so it cannot be exhausted. Therefore, the army was based on food and grass, and the war began with a miraculous strategy. The instruments and tools were the weapons for the war, and the material was the reserve for the war. So the country's difficulty lies in buying grain when the price was high, and the difficulty in fighting lies in long-distance transportation. If the attack was not successful, we should not rush to attack again, but consider all aspects. We can't fight three times in a row. We should did what we can. If we fight more times, we would spend more. Only by eliminating meaningless waste, could the country be stable easily; it was good for the country to eliminate incompetent generals. A general who good at attacking , the enemy did not know where he to defense; a general who good at defensiving, the enemy did not know where he was going to attack. So the generals who were good at attacking did not take pride in the strength of the soldiers, and the generals who were good at defending did not take pride in the soundness of the city. Therefore, it was not enough for a strong reason that the walls were tall and the moats were deep and wide; it was not enough for a strong reason that a strong and well armored soldier was strong. If the enemy intends to keep on defending, our army would attack places where they had no defense; if the enemy intends to send troops to the array, our army would attack places where they were weak by surprise. If both sides of the enemy and ourselves attack and defend each other, our army should carefully choose where to camp. When our army was attacking and the enemy was not moving, we should attack the enemy from the left and right. Measure how to encircle the enemy and attack the key parts of the enemy first. As a general, If he's not familiar with the city's defense and the time to start the war, there were many places and things to prepare, then simply defending would be thin. Should be prepared in all directions, How to attack when we were strong or when we were weak, how to rescue each other when we were brave and timid, how to cooperate with the former and the latter, how to take care of each other between the left and the right, like the long snake of Hengshan, which could take care of each other flexibly, was the way of combat rescue. In fact, they had planned carefully in advance and were familiar with geography, meteorology, the army, momentum and other aspects, this cannot be said in advance. A little discussion, we could know the gain and loss of this matter, know the safety and the danger of this matter, know how much this matter; control, compare, we could know the existence of this matter and the demise of the truth, know the pain and joy of this matter, know whether this matter was perfect and complete. Therefore, when fighting, we should take into account the survival of the soldiers and fight against the enemy who was about to collapse; we should avoid the enemy with strong strength and fight against the enemy with weak strength. When fighting in hills and hills, we can't attack from the lower part of the terrain to the higher part; when fighting by the water, we can't attack against the water; when fighting on the grass, we can't attack too deeply; when fighting on the plain, we can't fight hard, we should follow the weak part of the enemy; when fighting on the road, we should find that the other side was alone, and we should fight according to this idea. In these five cases, the method of using troops was to take advantage of the terrain. The success of war lies in the use of "potential", the failure comes from the leakage of stratagem, the hunger lies in the long-distance transportation, the thirst lies in the personal drilling of wells instead of using the enemy's well, the weariness lies in the annoyance and being harassed, the ease and relaxation lies in the silence, the doubt lies in not daring to send troops to fight, the confusion lies in seeing only a small benefit, the retreat lies in the penalty, the advance lies in the reward, the cowardice lies in forcing; strength lies in the use of "potential"; difficulty lies in being surrounded; fear lies in seeing the opponent arrive first; panic lies in hearing the call in the middle of the night; confusion lies in ambiguity, bad relations and different orders; confusion lies in losing the way; poverty lies in falling into the hopeless situation, failure lies in the sudden death of soldiers, and victory lies in planning ahead of time. So we designed banners and flags to let the soldiers see with their eyes; we use the sound of gongs and drums, let the soldiers hear, and set axes and axes as instruments to punish the soldiers for violating military orders. We used this majesty to let the soldiers unite. Make public the rules and orders so that the soldiers could abide by them, advocate rewards, guide their behaviors, and let them fight bravely against the enemy. Execution of penalties and beheadings to prevent the soldiers from cheating. During the day, we can't hear each other, only see and obey the command of the banners. In night combat, we can't see each other. The sound of the torch and the drum was the signal of command. If someone disobeys the order, let the punishment become the tool to carry out the order and discipline. If you did not know the nine convenient ways of terrain, you cannot know the nine ways to attack the enemy. Heaven had Yin and Yang, earth had shape and name, and man had belly and heart. If you know these three aspects, you could gain and deal with the gains and losses of marching. If you know the situation of the soldiers, you would know the situation of the enemy. If you did not know the situation of the soldiers, you would not know the situation of the enemy. If you battle, you would inevitably be in danger every time. So when attacking in battle, we ought to know in advance what the left and right soldiers think. The method of alienation should be discussed by the general himself, and the general should give priority to it. It's not that wise people didn't know how to use alienation, you can't use such a strategy if you're not a benevolent and wise person. If the plan of alienation was reasonable, it could be used in battle and the country could be protected for a long time. Therefore, war was to be prepared for survival, and only when it had to be fought. If it was quiet, there should be sufficient reasons for the troops to be quiet. If it was moving, there should be reasons for the troops to be majestic and powerful in momentum. We should not rely on the enemy's absence to feel safe, but on the fact that our army had no weak links and let the enemy can't attack us, so that we could be safe. Let our army get close to the battlefield and wait for the enemy coming far away; wait for the tired enemy with a quiet and leisure mind; let soldier with full meal wait the hungry enemy; wait for the weak enemy with a strong soldier; wait for the enemy stepping into the dead with a way of survival; wait for the less enemy with a large number of soldiers; wait for the enemy with a strong morale; wait for the enemy with an ambush waiting for the arrival. Neat banners and flags and loud war drums should be placed in front of the troops, when the war was over, they should be put away. We should strengthen and consolidate the forces and instruments that obstruct enemy in critical positions; we should manage them on the surface of the formation, entrust our generals with interests and honors, and encourage them; we should deal with the enemy in danger and make him weak. This was the way to run the army!

Reward and punishment Tenth

The right way to reward and punish was to reward the noble and punish the ugly. Reward could urge people to strive for the establishment of merit, and Punishment could stop wrongdoing. Rewards and penalties need to be fair and just. Reward needs to know why reward was carried out so that warriors could understand how to sacrifice their lives for reward; punishment needs to know why punishment was carried out so that evil behaviors would be forbidden and evil people would understand what to fear. Therefore, rewards cannot be given falsely or punished casually. If the reward was given to a person who had made a false report of his or her achievements, then the person who had made a real contribution would complain; if the person who should not be punished was punished, then the upright person would resent. Therefore, Sima Ziqi destroyed Zhongshan state because of the uneven distribution of mutton soup, and King Huai of Chu lost Chu state because he listened to the slanderous talk. Therefore, generals use the power of life and death to maintain their prestige. If the people who should be alive were killed, the people who should be dead not killed; anger would not check the details; there was no correct scale for reward and punishment; the rules and regulations were not fixed; exploit public offices for private gain; these were the five dangers of the country. If the rewards and punishments were not understood, there would be somebody disobedience in the prescribed system. Those who had to behead can't be forbidden to commit crimes if they were allowed to live. If people who should be alive were beheaded, the soldiers would flee. Angry didn't ask for details, the fight staff sometimes didn't punish, the reward and punishment were unclear, subordinates didn't work hard, the issued rules and regulations were not appropriate, laws and orders were not obeyed, exploit public offices for private gain, people had two minds. So if someone did something bad and didn't forbid it, everyone would follow suit; if a soldier escapes, the strength of the army would weaken; if the commanding order was not carried out, the army that meets the enemy would not be able to fight bravely. If subordinates didn't make efforts to build their own achievements, then leaders would not had strong assistance. If the law was not obeyed, there would be chaos and no one would deal with it. If people had thoughts of disloyalty, the country would be in danger. Therefore, we should formulate policies and measures to prevent crimes, everything in the daily life should be frugal, avoid luxury. Honest and upright people could manage prison, Incorruptible and fairness people could manage reward and punishment. If reward and punishment were not partial, people would be convinced even if they were sentenced to death. There were hungry people on the road and fat horses in the stables. This phenomenon was that all people had fled, but they were still on their own. They treat others very mean and treat themselves very well. So the monarch recruits first, then rewards, issues rules first, and then kills those who violate the rules. In this way, people would adhere to and abide by the rules like their relatives. They would love each other for fear of violating the rules. They would always act without stopping the order. If the reward and punishment were unfair, the loyal ministers would be executed without guilt, and the wicked ministers would be used because they had no credit. Reward could not avoid resentment and hatred, so Duke Huan got Guan Zhong's help; punishment and killing could not avoid his relatives, s o Zhou Gong Gong had a reputation for killing his younger brother. The book says: if there was no partiality and no privately forming a party, then the benevolent imperial power would be mighty; if there was no partiality and no partiality, then the benevolent imperial power would be plain. That's why.

Like and Angry Eleventh

Like and angry management methods, when you like, shouldn't like something that 's not worth the happy; when you angry, shouldn't angry something that't not worth angry, like and angry, we ought to distinguish different categories. Anger can't be aimed at people who didn't make mistakes; like, can't be aimed at people who were going to be killed; between like and anger, we can't avoid exploring the details. Like a person, can't connive this person's sin; angry a person, can't kill an innocent person. Like and angry things, could not happen and implement casually. In behavior, if general deals with his own private affairs in the name of the public, did so, his subordinates' idea of perform meritorious deeds would be dispelled. The general can 't vent personal anger when handle official business, because the war was to rely on everyone to unite as one, if the generals vent their personal resentment and lead the army to fight, it would fail. When dealing with war, the general needs to fight when he was angry. He can't be happy again, because when he was happy, he might withdraw his army. When he was happy, he can't be angry again. Because he was angry, he might send out troops and cannot fight back, he cannot promise and then deny in succession; therefore, he needs to try fair means before resorting to force. Because the personal anger, the first to start a war, would inevitably be followed by failure; the first because of the personal anger of the general, and sent troops to fight, would inevitably regret, inadvertently angry for a while, and might let their own demise. Therefore, a gentleman was mighty but not vicious, hate but not angry, worried but not afraid, happy but not revealed. If something worthy of anger happens, then use your might. After the display of power, the criminal law and penalties would be implemented; after the criminal law and penalties were implemented, the behavior of people committing crimes would be blocked. If the general didn't wield authority, the criminal law and punishment did not work, the ugliness of the people would not be dealt with, so the country would inevitably perish.

Governance Confusion Twelfth

The way to deal with chaos was what Guan Zhong said in his article "provincial officials", was the responsibility of officials at all levels, was the duty of officials at all levels to discard external modifications and retain high moral quality, that's all. If the officials at all levels did not perform their duties seriously and continuously, there would be chaotic and tangled incidents; if small and wrong things were not stopped, disaster would inevitably occur. There were three kinds of ethic relations: the example of a monarch as a minister, the example of a father as a son, and the example of a husband as a wife; there were six kinds of human and kinsfolk relations: filial piety for father and father's relatives, fraternity for brothers, courtesy for mother and mother's relatives, respect for rules and order for clansmen, respect for teachers, and feelings for friends. If these relations were not straightened out, then great confusion would inevitably arise. Therefore, the people who govern the country can't be smooth without certain rules, the party can't had certain rules, the roots can't lose the treetops, and the government can't lose the proper systems and methods. In this way, everything could succeed and the achievements could be maintained. The relations among the three armies were numerous and complicated, and everything lies in the internal "reason". The wise monarch governs three principles and six disciplines, and governs the country first, then, combing three principles and six disciplines; first, sorting out laws and regulations, then punishments; first, sorting out near things, then distant things; first, dealing with internal things, then external things; first, dealing with essence, then ending things; first, dealing with great harm, then small harm; first, dealing with great things, Deal with small things later; deal with your own problems first, and deal with others' problems later. So we had the outline first, and then we had the details. After the order and rules were issued, the punishment could be implemented; if the immediate affairs were handled, the distant affairs might be stable; if the internal affairs were straightened out, the external affairs might be correct; if the internal affairs were straightened out, the ending would be straightened out; if the harmful matters were dealt with, the harmful matters would be converged; if the major matters were dealt with, the minor matters would be natural However, if we follow the example, if we were honest above, we would be honest below; if we had no problems with ourselves, then others would naturally respect us, which was the principle of governing our country.

Military Orders Thirteenth

The method of management, such as regulations and orders, was to educate the lower level. As a superior, if you didn't speak what didn't conform to the laws and regulations, if you didn't did things what didn't conform to the regulations, your superior's words and deeds, would be subordinate attention and follow-up. Therefore, if you make a mistake and were released, but you had to teach others to abide by the law, this was "Violation of Decree"; if you act correctly, and you teach others to abide by the law, this was "Compliance with Decrees". Therefore, the monarch first makes his behavior conform to the rules and regulations, and then orders others to obey. If one's behavior was not correct, it was difficult to ask others to obey orders; if the order was not obeyed, it was easy to cause disorder. So as the monarch's correct method, was the provisions of the command in front of the punishment and death at the back; if not education and training of soldiers, and let the soldiers go to war, was to give up the lives of soldiers. The important thing is, let the soldiers practice the rules and tactics of combat. There were five methods. First, let the soldiers be familiar with the rules of changing flags as command signs. From forward, backward, turn left turn right, all the changes come from the flags. Second, let the soldiers be familiar with the sound of war drums and gongs. They need to hear the sounds of action, stillness, attack and stop. Third, let the soldiers be familiar with the severity of punishment and the benefits of rewards; fourth, let the soldiers practice the methods of using five weapons to prepare for battle; fifthly, let the soldiers practice and be familiar with turn circle; this was known as the five rules. There were different reasons and regulations for making military orders public. On the left was the green dragon flag, on the right was the white tiger flag, on the front was the Zhuque flag, on the back was the Xuanwu flag, and on the center was the Xuanyuan flag. The position of the commander of the army was that the left guard holds a spear, the right guard holds a sword and halberd, the front guard holds a Hengge, the back guard holds a bow and crossbow, and the center was set with flags and drums. When the war flag shakes, all of them should obey the orders, when they hear the sound of the war drum, they would move forward, when they hear the sound of the Gong, they would stop moving forward, and they should obey the commands of the flag and the drum, which was the principle of the five arrangements. The method of arranging troops was mainly flag and drum. If drum call was once, would raise the green flag and form a vertical array. If drum call was twice, would raise the red flag and form a assault array. If drum call was thrice, would raise the yellow flag and form a square array. If drum call was four times, would raise the white flag and form a circular array. If drum call was five times, would raise the black flag and form a curved array. The vertical array represents "Wood"; the assault array represents "Fire"; the square array represents "Soil"; the circular array represents "Gold"; the curved array represents "Water". This was a five element array of water, wood, gold, fire and earth. It's cyclic, complementary and changeable. Water makes wood, wood makes fire, fire makes earth, earth makes gold, gold makes water. Water conquers fire, fire conquers gold, gold conquers wood, wood conquers earth, and soil conquers water. When the unity of opposites breaks the relative balance or unity, things would incline to one side and change; for the sake of balance, make and conquer should be controlled by each other; when they can't restrain each other, when the balance was broken, things would had new changes. For a five element array, For a five element array, five people in a group should protect each other. Take five people as a group and set up a team leader; five groups as a division and set up a division leader; five divisions as a branch and set up a branch leader; five branches as a crowd and set up a crowd leader; five crowds as a area leader and set up a area leader; five areas as an army and set up a army leader. In this way, it forms an all-round allocation of military personnel. Operations need to act according to the battlefield situation, be sure to had control. Small soldiers hold spears, tall soldiers hold bows and crossbows, strong soldiers hold flags, brave soldiers hold drums and gongs, weak soldiers let them provide food and grass, smart people let them plan and make ideas. Small teams and small teams refer to each other and take care of each other. Five and five protect each other. If drum call was once, they would organize and practice; if drum call was twice, they would form a formation; if drum call was thrice, they would eat; if drum call was four times, they would gather; if drum call was five times, they would set out. Follow the drums of war and the sound of the golden gong and hold up the war flag. The soldiers march in turn. After drum call was thrice, the flags fly. Soldiers who were the first to attack in front would be rewarded. The soldiers that run away when going into battle were beheaded and shown to the public. This was the order.

Beheading Fourteenth

Beheading measures could be described as a management approach for about disobeying command behavior. There were seven methods. One was to despise the order, the other was to neglect the order, the third was to steal, the fourth was to cheat, the fifth was to betray, the sixth was to make trouble, the seventh was to delay the military opportunity. This was a ban on the management of the army. If what should be decided, but without making it immediately, it would inevitably cause disaster. Set up the executioners to deterrence the soldiers who did not obey the orders and behead them to the public. Military laws and regulations were different. If the crime was light and the punishment was heavy, the order can't be violated any more, and those who violate it would be beheaded. Those who didn't arrive at the appointed time; those who didn't advance when they hear the drums; those who take the loose opportunity to keep; those who shirk fighting and stop without permission; those who could get close to the battlefield at first, and then get away from it later; Those who call his name, who didn't answer; those who did not drive vehicles according to orders and did not wear armor; those who didn't prepare the weapons; all these behaviors belong to contempt of military command. Those who despise military command ought to be beheaded and shown to the public. Those who receive orders and did not convey them; those who convey them incompletely; those who confuse officials and soldiers, those who did not listen to gongs and drums; those who did not look at banners and flags; all these were acts of neglecting military orders, and those who neglect military orders ought to be beheaded and shown to the public. The food eaten was not the food provided by the public; the officers did not economize on the use of troops; taxes and rewards were not even; they teach each other privately; they obtain property that did not belong to them; they borrow money from others and did not repay it; those who injure the people and falsely claim military exploits; all these behaviors belong to the "stealing army", and those who steal the army behead to the public. Changing one's own name, unclean clothes, broken flags, incomplete gongs and drums, no rubbing of weapons, no tenacity of instruments, The arrow had no feathers, the crossbow had no bowstring, and the law was not enforced. All these actions belong to the deceiving army, and the deceiving army ought to be beheaded and shown to the public. those who hears the sound of drums and did not move forward, those who hears the sound of the golden gong and did not stop, those who press down the flag and did not ambush, those who raises the flag and did not standing up, those who disobeying the command; those who demanding to move forward but backward; those who walk crosswise or randomly, those who break bows and crossbows, those who retreat and did not fight, those who should turn left and right, those who didn't did their best to help the wounded soldiers and leading to the death of soldiers, those who find excuses by themselves They retreated; These actions were against the military command. Those who violate the military command were beheaded and shown to the public. When the troops set out, they did not march in line, scrambling, crowding each other, making noise, vehicles and horses connecting with each other, clogged traffic arteries, the soldiers behind could not move forward, calling loudly, hearing no orders, the order of march was out of control, were accidental injury by weapons , not in accordance with the military common sense, which was disrupt the military array, disrupt the military array ought to be beheaded and shown to the public. At the campsite, ask the local guide, let close friends follow, protect each other's diet, and did not exceed the order and rules. When the camp where stationed, let the local villagers act as a guide, let close confidants follow, eat together or take care of each other, and did not exceed the order and rules. Those who forcibly enter other teams; those who disturb and delay order; those who can't stop after shouting; those who didn't walk in and out of the barracks through the gate; those who didn't report the accident by themselves; those who did not report after the evil thing had happened; those Who drinks alcohol without permission; those who loudly say the password and leak the secret; those who doubt or confuse the officers, These all about delaying the army, those who delaying the army ought to be beheaded and shown to the public. All this, after the beheading, everything was relatively smooth.

Being Prepared for Eny Eventualities Fifteenth

The strategy of being prepared for any eventualities was the way to think about the immediate things and worry about the long-term things. If you didn't worry about the long-term things, the immediate things would cause trouble. So a gentleman (man of complete virtue) thinks about the problem from the perspective of position responsibility. Thinking, was plan things correctly; worried, was a way to ponder problem and solve problem. If you were not in a certain position, you would not plan the management strategy from the perspective of the responsibilities of the position; if you were not in a certain position, you would not worry about the solutions. Big things were caused by disasters, small things were caused by simple troubles.

Therefore, if you want to think about the good side of this matter, you ought to think about the harm of this matter; if you want to think about making this matter a success, you ought to think about what to did if you fail. So the nine story platform, though tall, would had a collapse day. Therefore, looking up at the high place, we can't ignore its bottom; seeing the bright side of the future, we can't ignore the dim side. Therefore, when Duke mu of Qin attacked Zheng, several people in Jianshu and xuangao saw the harm of doing so. When the king of Wu accepted Xishi, Wu Zixu saw that the consequences of doing so were bound to fail. After Yu's monarch accepted jasper and fine horse, Gong Zhiqi saw that Jin was going to eliminate Yu. When Song Xianggong trained his soldiers and horses, simaziyu saw that Song Xianggong's conceit would lead to the defeat and humiliation of the song state. These intelligent people think very well, so to speak, they think very clearly and see for a long time. So follow the track of the defeated army, follow the track of mire, stay close and move forward, where could we reach? Therefore, the overlord inherited by the state of Qin could not catch up with the way of governing the country of Yao and shun. So danger was produced when it was safe, death was produced when it was alive, and chaos was produced when it was managed. At the beginning, a gentleman could see how things would develo. When he sees the beginning, he could predict the result. Disasters can't happen for no reason. This was a question for thinking and worrying.

Secretly Self-examination Sixteenth

Observing and thinking in private, just like something, was just feeling and understanding its meaning. If the external was hurt and attacked, the internal would feel lonely; if the superior was confused, the subordinate would doubt; if the superior lack of common sense, the people who could help him would not be reused; if the superior was confused, the accuracy would be lost; if the accuracy was lost, the people who could help him would not be used; if the superior was confused, the people who could see the problem would lose the accuracy; if the accuracy was lost, the people who could make a plan would be disorderly; if the plan was disorderly, the country would be in danger, and the country would be. Therefore, people who think about problems ought to think about the long term. Only when they think about the long term could they be safer. People who didn't think would be in danger. Rich people were complacent; poor people lose the opportunity to grow crops; excessive greed would inevitably lead to too much waste; collect a lot of food, but did not give poor people a lot of money; if there was a disaster, there would be a major calamity; use up their own wealth to buy things; no credit and their own tyranny; trouble would annoy people; slack would cause troubles. If the boat was sloshing, it might enter the water; if the bag was broken, there would be scattered things in it, and it would become empty; if the mountain forest was very small, there would be no wild animals; if the water was too shallow, there would be no fish; if the trees were weak, there would be no bird's nest; if the wall was broken, the house might collapse; if the dike was broken, the water would flow out; if the people walk too fast, they might fall; if they walk steadily, they might walk slowly; if they climb on the dangerous places, they were relatively superficial; people who walk on thin ice would be afraid; they might be submerged when they walk into a channel with water; they need to ferry when they meet water, but they can't cross without a boat, and those who lose their partners need long-term consideration; they need clear rewards and punishments to save time and effort; dishonest people lose credit. If the lips were splited, the teeth would feel cold; If the outer fur falls off, the inner cortex becomes thin. He who was partial to himself and speaks recklessly was prone to misfortune. Those who were good at planning were easy to win, and those who plot country well without relying on the army; those who were good at leading the army could command the army without relying on the arrangement of troops; those who were good at arrangement of troops could simply arrange troops without relying on fighting; those who were good at fighting could not fail; those who were good at summarizing the lessons of failure could not be annihilated. Before, sages governed the country, so that the people could had a safe place to live, so that the people could work happily, so that the people would not attack each other and fight, that was to say, a ruler who was good at running a country did not depend on the army. As Shun amended the law and punishment, Gao Tao, as a wise grand master, assisted the monarch to formulate five punishments and five religions. No one violated the law and there was no object for the punishment to be carried out. That was to say, those who were good at commanding the army did not need to arrange troops. For example, the great Yu's crusade against the Miao family was unsuccessful, and the Shun's dance was to dry the feathers, moving people with morality, and the Miao family's automatic allegiance. That was to say, those who were good at arranging troops and arranging the array won without starting a war. Like Duke Huan of Qi conquering the powerful state of Chu in the South and Beirong in the north, this was the case that the man who was good at fighting could be invincible. For example, after King Zhao of Chu was occupied by the enemy, he fled to the state of Qin for help, and finally returned to the state. This was an example of those who were good at summing up the lessons of failure.

The Generals Commandments

The book says: if you tease a gentleman, you can't make a gentleman serve you sincerely; if you insult a villain, you can't make a villain did his best for yourself. Therefore, the essentials of marching and fighting ought to be to win the hearts of brave soldiers, to reward and punish them clearly, to combine one relaxation with another, to help each other with hardness and softness, to train and educate their subordinates to abide by the rules and understand the etiquette. First, soldiers should be benevolent, then they should be witty and brave. When it's quiet, it's like a fish lurking under the water. When it's moving, it's like a marmot running. When it's losing its position, it's involved. If they too harsh and excessive, it's necessary for them to be restrained. When cheering, use banners; when admonishing, use gongs and drums. When retreating, it moves like a mountain, majestic but not disorderly; when advancing, it moves like wind and rain, fast and unimpeded. When attacking, destroy the enemy like a crash. They should come down like a tiger in a joint operation. If the enemy was pressing hard, we should learn to tolerate it and then looking for combat opportunities. Use small profits to lure and confuse the enemy. When the enemy was in confusion, take the opportunity to attack. Despicable people should find ways to make them arrogant. When the enemy unite and find a way to separate them. When the enemy was strong, we ought to find a way to make them weak. When there was danger, try to make the soldiers feel safe. When there was fear, try to make the soldiers happy. When some soldiers want to betray, we should adopt a soft policy to resolve conflicts. Those who had been wronged should be given the opportunity to complain. If there were overbearing people, we should try to restrain them. If there were weak and small people, we need to find ways to support them. If we meet strategic people, we need to find ways to get close to them. If we meet someone who offers slander, we should try to restrain them. Those who had seized property should be rewarded with some. We didn't need twice as many soldiers to attack the weak enemy. Don't look down on the enemy by relying on many people. Don't neglect others because of their ability. Don't be swayed by flattery. Plan before you act. It was calculated that we could win before we fight. Obtain property and did not allow individuals to take it without permission. The capture of the enemy's children should not be allowed to be left for personal use. If the generals could did so, and the orders were strict, and the soldiers were willing to fight hard, then you would be able to win without firing a shot, and the soldiers were willing to desperate.